WAITING FOR THE DOG TO SLEEP

WAITING FOR THE DOG TO SLEEP

Jerzy Ficowski

Translated from the Polish by
Soren A. Gauger & Marcin Piekoszewski

TWISTED SPOON PRESS • PRAGUE • 2006

*This publication has been funded by the
Book Institute – the ©POLAND Translation Program*

INSTYTUT KSIĄŻKI

©POLAND

CONTENTS

WAITING FOR THE DOG TO SLEEP

The Artificial Hen, or the Gravedigger's Lover

This is the town I know best. Tamed after a long period of intimacy, this is the only town that has shed every threat it once held. I perceive this town instinctively, without the need to understand it or explain it to myself. And it was right here, in an ordinary late autumn, in this very place! . . .

During office hours, the middle of the workday, in the deserted square: the squawk of a chicken. A squawk one hundred times more terrifying than a normal cluck. Violent gusts of wind sweep over the loose snow. The hen lifts its sumptuously feathered neck into the air and squawks. The neck lengthens for that squawk, as it grows it becomes thinner and thinner, more exposed, like a stiff branch. Now it is only the occasional red feather that flutters on its bare, taut skin, like the last of the autumn leaves. The hen runs left, then right. Struggling in the expanse of snow, it falls silent for a moment, contracts its neck, buries it under its wing, and hitting the invisible wall of its fear it suddenly gets stuck in one spot and draws out its neck to squawk again.

The perpetrator of the uproar jumps out from behind a house on the corner: a second hen, smaller, moving in long, nimble leaps, without a sound. Every leap provokes a squawk from the other hen, stretching its neck to its outer limits. In one more moment the neck will tear itself off, like a slingshot pulled too far.

I suddenly notice that the silent hen isn't exactly leaping: it's the gusts of wind that are carrying it so violently from place to place. I also notice that the silent hen is in fact a hen-shaped doll, sewn together with bunches of down on artificial goose-feather legs and tied at the stomach with string. It's an artificial hen, not subject to any easily anticipated biological laws. Before fear grips me entirely, I have to catch the Artificial Hen.

I chase after it. The squawks of the frightened hen, already far out of sight, ascend in scale. Carried by the wind, the Artificial Hen leaps over a freshly dug ditch and beyond the mound of earth in a single bound.

I'm in the ditch and would like to get out of it, but I am stopped by a child who says: "Calm down, stay put. There are municipal excavations being done all over town, a whole labyrinth of them. We are in one of the excavations. The road workers and the cable workers left long ago. So they've called in all the gravediggers from the surrounding cemeteries to do the work with their own shovels. Calm down, leave the Artificial Hen alone. She's the Gravedigger's lover; you'd never get away with it."

Fine, I'll calm down. I'll back off. The child whispers a warning: "The Gravedigger is patrolling along the ditch. I should hide before he sees me." I lie down on the floor of the ditch, right beside a ceramic wall with an oval opening. These walls partition the excavation site every couple of meters or so, evidently forming the base of some kind of underground installation. So as not to be observed through the oval opening in the wall, the child covers it with something found in the ditch, the same color, size, and shape as the wall.

The child fits the oval of baked clay into the wall, and as I lie on my back I shudder at the thought of the approaching Gravedigger, that he might notice our meddling. I comfort myself that even if he were to see me he would know nothing about my aborted chase after the Artificial Hen. Cold comfort: gravediggers, after all, bury the dormant. And so he will kill me by covering me with earth, not in the name of jealous revenge, but simply out of his gravedigger's duty.

Unnoticed, I crawl out of the excavation site and

escape. The outskirts are already entirely deserted, I might be the last resident to leave town. I can still get aboard the one means of transportation: a vehicle normally used to cart packages on railway platforms. I take my place among a few other coatless people who are randomly and colorfully dressed. We start silently moving along a smooth, snow-covered road by a river. The road slopes gently and we rush down, alongside the river, racing the current. Instead of a motor, it's the river that is roaring, and the man at the winch regulates the roar's intensity. Fog impairing our visibility, we pick up speed.

And then a time came when I returned to the town, but the town was no longer there. All that was left were houses reduced to cinders and bunches of feathers tossed about in the air, feathers from ripped bedding and pillows. A woman is collecting them in a pail. She takes a look at me and says: "I live on Czaprak Street. It's in the suburbs, the house was spared. You ordered some summer pants from us. They're ready."

I go with the woman. In the lonely tailor's workshop I pick up the pants I ordered before all this took place. They're a few centimeters too short. Could I have grown? They promise they'll do them over again: they'll sew on some cuffs and the pants will be just right. I pay. The woman and her two children are using the collected feathers to sew small artificial hens.

The Passing Settlement

I don't know and have never known its name. But this settlement is easy to recognize by its brevity, its rapid passing, almost at the very moment of greeting it we must bid it farewell. The train carries us past too quickly for it to be counted among places graced with topographical names; it is doubtless just one of those minor attractions organized for us, the long-distance travelers, by the State Railway, in the interest of alleviating boredom.

I have seen it repeatedly, I have even measured its distance: it stretches alongside the tracks for sixteen quick clacks of the wheels; by the seventeenth it is already gone, and only versts of empty meadows run smooth in its wake. I'm not even sure if it's only on the Warsaw-Białystok line that I've seen it or somewhere else as well. I get the feeling that I always pass it, no matter where I'm going, on those parts of the journey where the train has gathered the most speed, halfway between two distant stations.

This passing settlement has never been my destination, I will never interrupt my journey there. Even now, when I think back, it is difficult for me to recall how it sprawls across a plain among trees stiffly rooted in the motionless earth. I remember the green plumes of its close-up acacias slipping by with a faraway forest as a backdrop, momentarily trying to follow in the train's wake, with the skittish acacias scurrying in the opposite direction. In the end, however, the forest stays with its settlement, like the shore of an island diminishing into the distance, all awash with the violent current of our speeding passage.

Due to its inaccessibility, the settlement is the subject of my boldest hypotheses and conjectures, which are all the more true in that they are unverifiable. Ephemeral, summoned into existence in the space of an instant behind a train window, it confirms all of my suppositions, every speculation; it cannot, after all, say anything to contradict them. And so, initially featureless, ready to shoulder any interpretation, the settlement is gradually penciled in with the meaning I have nominated for it, and yet it is capable of renouncing this meaning at any moment in the name of my changing whims.

I imagine old Miłowicka lives in any one of those cottages.

She has varicose veins, likes to sit by the window, never leaves the house. She vanished once, the last of my nannies. You can't see her behind the racing thicket of acacias, but she's there, eyes fixed on the sky and the railway tracks. For her, the train falls into the category of atmospheric phenomena, a close relative of the storm, especially at night. It's preceded by the light from the reflectors, like a flash of lightning, and then the thunder swells and gradually softens into the darkness. From behind the rattling pane, Miłowicka thanks Providence that the storm has again sailed past at a distance. Behind a small orchard there's a hangar for gliders from the times when a special train would stop here once a week. Now the hangar is watched by an old man the settlement calls Sergeant Józiuk; I don't know if this is his first or last name. The sergeant is missing all his fingers on his left hand, and he spends his days taming wild horses, which he stables in the old hangar. It was back in September '39, after a skirmish, that the surviving horses of the 7th Cavalry Regiment, some of whom were wounded, made it to the forest. Whereupon the mares foaled and foaled some more, breeding these wild offspring, which are very hard to break. Sergeant Józiuk will tell you that he once came across an old mare, it was still carrying a rotten saddle and bits of an officer's boot in one of the stirrups. No doubt it was the Mother herself, the oldest of the wild lineage.

Or not. Isn't it oddly symptomatic that only the trees of

the settlement run out to meet the train? That not once has a grubby little boy turned up, not even for the blink of an eye, to greet us with a wave of his hand over his head? And the smoke trailing over the settlement is never more than the smoke from the locomotive; chimneys there do not smoke. Small wonder: the settlement died out in the 40s during the cholera epidemic. And there's no hangar there, just a cholera graveyard, completely dilapidated. People from the distant Roman Catholic parish avoid this place. Cholera epidemics are a thing of the past, the word only serves as a curse.* This is why the distant neighbors of this ghost settlement take the local dead for the godless adherents of some blasphemous cult. The houses are empty and looted; crows and jackdaws use them for nesting. For one-hundred-and-some-odd years a lack of transport vehicles has made taking down the buildings and carting off the timber not worth the trouble; at any rate, it would only be good for kindling. The miserable remains of the settlement are deteriorating, only the acacias are running wild, and in June the heady fragrance of their blossoms drifts through the open windows of the trains.

I pass by there at various times of the year, but I see the settlement only in summer, or autumn at the latest. It's not as though at other times of the year it isn't in its usual place, but in winter a thick layer of hoarfrost obscures the view. And yet the settlement is there, you can be sure, not covered in snow, but always green, thanks to a very warm trade wind that blows through. Hence, an endless vacation. Groups of vacationers lie under the well-sweeps on colorful lawn chairs, some stroll in their pajamas along the railway embankment. The settlement doesn't run pensions or bed-and-breakfast inns, everything operates more simply: every shed, spare room, or attic serves the seasonal residents. They mostly come from homes that no longer exist, from districts and towns razed to the ground during the war. Thus the holiday season lasts much longer in these parts, the days spent in reading old newspapers and telling fortunes from acacia leaves. The local landlords have offered every last nook of their domiciles to the arrivals and have nested themselves in dugouts that look more like badger holes. A certain diversity does exist in the sunny monotony. In the fire station, which resembles the old hangar, once they even selected a Miss Settlement. She is Rebecca Klein, copper-haired, her skin also tanned copper, in a tight-fitting dress, green as verdigris. She sits in a lawn chair in the sun, her eyes are closed and through her eyelids she sees colors. It's nice here. She no longer recalls if she once had siblings or even an uncle somewhere. She's completely absorbed in the colors under her eyelids: on a big orange background is an upside-down turquoise heart with a violet fringe. Things are prettiest behind Rebecca Klein's closed eyes.

It's good that the train doesn't stop here. The desire that it would just for once make an exception, perhaps due to some unforeseen damage to the rails, left me some time ago. I know the settlement just from the bat of an eye, I don't want its annihilation, I wish it well. Even if fate were to decree that, contrary to my desire, there would be a forced stop, compelling me to wander beyond that first row of acacias, I wouldn't be able to communicate with anyone in the settlement. It is, after all, inhabited only by foreigners. They came passing through decades ago, in sealed boxcars, from as far away as the Pyrenees. Happily forgotten at the side of the tracks, they built a passing settlement out of railway ties and old boxcars on the wasteland . . . and somehow they are able to live. From the window of a second-class compartment, I wish them well.

Old-World Entomology

B ehind the dark windowpane, moths fluttering in place, mothlings, winglets, mousselines, a full calligraphic alphabet of the night. They are drawn to my light in a whisper of wings.

Sometimes a gong: a hoverer or a coleopterous scarabeid suddenly collides with the glass. A short series of these collisions and the panes blacken like a chalkboard that has had its letters erased. Then all grows quiet except for the monotonous rustle: this night will again inscribe on a black background hundreds of its verses, full of elaborate flourishes, like the signature of Emil Wedel.* Entomology is old-world.

I open the window. At once I find myself in the center

of a tickling, windless blizzard, amidst flutterings and knockings on the ceiling and walls. I make a futile attempt to beat off the whirling clouds; I want to escape the lunatic insectarium, but then a pair of enormous, flapping insects descends into the room. One of them is shaggy, with wings sharp as a swallow's, flapping only infrequently, gliding without a quiver, turning precisely measured circles, figure-eights and ellipses. The second one has open-work lace wings which gently fan in its flight around the lamp. It is slower and somewhat awkward.

Then I realize: it's Grandfather Karol's moustache and Granny Łucja's ruffles. They settle on my palm. I quickly bring them to a neighboring room where it's dark. I know them from some ruddy photographs on stiff cardboard with the golden signature of a master photographer from Kiev. How far they must have flown to get here, a distance of 800 kilometers and sixty years. Staggering the powers of phototaxis and the memory of the deceased.

I can't say if they flew from Gorczaków or Taraszcza. Whatever the case, certainly from the direction of Gorczaków. I place them on the tablecloth in the half-light. I burn candles, as I'm out of oil for the old vintage lamp and feel as though electric light would be out of place. But what can I give apart from these candles? Fragmentary and reduced to such residual forms, what could they desire?

At the edge of the table, in the radiance of the candles,

they whir, motionless, yet still full of wind, vibrating their wings with miniature shivers. Yes, forget about tales of Gorczaków which don't concern them any more. Forget about the samovar, about Seweryn the cowherd who wove hats, about Pejsach the red-haired carpenter, about Granny Susana the "all-knowing" crone and her ape-man Ołeksy Basaraba, about the dark Cossack and labor-convict Sawa Moroza, who brought cedar nuts for the children, about forests, about *pampuszki** with garlic, about everything.

Those two nocturnal winglets are all that remain of the whole affair. Dear God, how long can one remain a particle of the non-existent? Finally, they are starting to become something, anything, at least unto themselves. Even odds and ends have an instinct for self-preservation. There are no hard feelings, Grandparents. I'll bring some phlox from the garden, all moths love phlox.

When I return I stand in the doorway with my bouquet. My guests are gone. The candle flames frizzle, there's a burning smell. Ashen scraps fall to the tablecloth in flaming flickers, rising for just one more moment in the heated air, as if attempting flight with some last vestiges of strength.

Recreation with the Paralytics

What I know about the wall is my present knowledge. At one time I would stand before it, with its complex and multi-directional inscriptions, like Champollion* facing the hieroglyphics, before, in their silent ornamentation, they laid bare their age-old meaning. I studied chalk-drawn circles with vertically marked diameters, circles overgrown with thorns of concentric rays, signs of secret and vulgar knowledge. I was not among the initiated . . . this writing in scratched plaster, public like a municipal bulletin, was in its *essence* inaccessible. I passed it daily on the way to the primary school run by Mrs. Tomaszewska, a retired teacher. She was venerable and God-fearing and wore an immemorial gray chignon, which had been salvaged, evidently, from the horrors of the January Uprising.* She squeezed a private three-grade school into the few rooms of her first-floor apartment.

After our difficulties in fathoming the alphabet, the whole class took a long recess in the garden, which was never officially in that part of town. A side entrance through a courtyard gate took us there. We were meant to rest, breathe some fresh air, and in the autumn we collected chestnuts. I had already caught on to reading and writing, the lessons were useless, and yet I would get fatigued . . . not because of the alphabet, but because of the centuries-old instruments and knick-knacks that filled Mrs. Tomaszewska's apartment. Contrary to appearances, it was these things that ran the lessons, that prepared us, the pupils, for the past. And I was afraid that the inevitable result of that education, its single effect, would be the gray venerability that would envelop me in its growth as I stood at the very threshold of life, barricaded on all sides by misshapen tables with incrusted tops, amidst recollections confused with fantasy, recollections that cost thousands of paper rubles, no longer in circulation and found astray between the pages of missals and breviaries. Of course, I wasn't consciously aware of this overwhelming danger, it was rather felt instinctually. And so, plunged in concerns which warded off the tedium, I awaited the time to take a walk as though it were the redemption.

It seems to me — though I may be mistaken with the passing of time — that it was forever autumn in the garden, and regardless of the season, whenever I went, there were always freshly-fallen chestnuts on the grass. Some jumped from their bursting shells when they fell and shined with fresh lacquer like the round wooden handles on Mrs. Tomaszewska's mahogany cupboard. On one side, however, was the blind patch of white, the stamp of its infancy. Others leaned ever-so-gently through the chink in their thorny green shells . . . it was these in fact that kept reminding me of the marks on the wall. And it was right during the never-ending chestnut season that one day they forgot about me and I was left behind, alone in the garden. My pockets packed with a loot of chestnuts, I looked about fearfully, seeing things around me for the first time. Until then our teachers had done the looking for us, I had focused my attention downwards, into the grass, into the den of fallen chestnuts, and it must have been for this reason that I had decided the garden was endless. Now for the first time I noticed its extents, not so very distant, its limitations. Behind a pair of imposing chestnut trees the front of a two-story home was visible, bearing the inscription HOME FOR THE ELDERLY AND PARALYZED. A herd of pensioners gathered by the garden entrance, on crutches and in wheelchairs, as though afraid of the garden and the constant threat of a chestnut missile, which would be signaled by a scuffling in the leaves high above before it came rocketing down. At the nearby chapel doors, nuns were moving about, creatures with white-winged heads, like headwinged cherubs descending upon Christmas trees. From all three sides, for the garden was triangular, rose the blind, sparsely-plastered walls of buildings, and it was only thanks, perhaps, to the mighty dam of chestnut trees that they were not able to trample the garden entirely, to fuse into a single wall.

Suddenly I realized that what was called the local air, fresh air, was in reality not even the smell of rot, or a wilted waft of October, it was the fragrance of sanctity, a sacral climate. In that aroma of inertia and samaritanism the slackened gestures of the ill, with the support of the nuns' hieratic movements, acted out autumn's ongoing mystery play and celebrated the *roraty* service* of the chestnut dusk. The part of the enclosure that separated the garden from Lviv Street was on the inside completely overgrown with vines and sparrows, whose chirping married with the choral songs from the chapel, and perhaps even stood in for the choirboys' bells, which were unnecessary in these circumstances. A multicolored light filtered into the garden through a small, oval stained-glass window; it grew more and more chilly; over the garden's secreted air-pocket billowed a mountain of metropolitan smoke.

Down the lane that ran straight to the Institution doors came a figure in an armchair on two big wheels. A girl with a colorful kerchief on her head, her inert legs tucked under a rug. With one hand she turned the crank which moved the chair forward, while the other picked up chestnuts along the way. She had very beautiful hands: slender and pale with long slim fingers. She smiled and handed me about a dozen. My pockets were already filled to the brim. I took the gifts, but as there was nowhere to put them I held the chestnuts in my cupped hands. I felt awful that she had to bend over, that my full hands couldn't help her. I was entirely defenseless against her charitable and crippled obligingness. It wasn't her handicap that bothered me, but my defenselessness, disabled with an overload of chestnuts, heavier for the added burden of gratitude. I hugged the handfuls of her generosity close to me, more paralyzed than she was. The awareness was seeping into my head that I hadn't been left here by chance, that here I was becoming an able-bodied ward of the Institution, a ward so advanced in his paresis that he required support even from his livelier companions in distress. I was a little boy, after all, there wasn't much I could do, and now . . . I can do nothing.

The girl, turning circles around me in her chair, went on with her collecting. I couldn't take one more gift, or even reach out my hand. She started putting a few chestnuts by herself into my small jacket pocket, which was still empty. I could not have imagined that her hands, so white, could burn, that they were so hot! Thank you! Thank you! I yelled, almost in tears, throwing the remainder of the chestnuts into my shirt and running for the chapel's stained-glass window. But just then its colors dampened and the garden grew even darker. I wove through the trees, passing the same hollowed-out chestnut tree with the severed branch time and again. The mark left by that white hand was still burning, refusing to cool off, the heat was intensifying, sending a rush of palpitations through my body.

When I had at last groped my way to the gate and run into the street, I saw the long-familiar wall, and its pictorial writing suddenly became accessible, shamelessly legible in the light of the streetlamps. It was, after all, the wall adjacent to the garden, on the side facing the street. From the interior it was sanctified by the acolyte responses of the sparrows, restrained through suffering and prayer, disinfected from sins . . . and here it went through furious recompenses, the rash-like suffusion of venereal stigmata, signs of fictitious rapes, the stipulated alphabet of the idolaters of the orgasm. All this is my present knowledge, then merely intuited, though the inscriptions essentially concealed their profoundly disturbing contents. I instinctively reached into my pocket for a piece of chalk, but couldn't find it among all the chestnuts. I started dumping them out and I noticed that they bore no trace of their lacquered shine: they were shrunken and shriveled, not even pleasant to touch.

The ave-bell sounded from behind the wall, the evening

call a signal to rest, for nighttime silence. I looked about; there was no one on the streets for as far as the eye could see. I took out the chalk from the bottom of my emptied pocket and, in the center of the wall . . . right next to the radiant, crossed-out circle, I hastily drew a white, five-fingered sign, an emblem of sudden comprehension. I returned home with larcenous and stealthy footsteps, and the following day was already winter, white and absolute. We stayed in class for recess, spending all the school hours amidst Mrs. Tomaszewska's chesterfields and display cabinets. It was too chilly for a walk, and in any case, there was no garden to walk in; in its place, at the three ends of the earth, sprawled an old nineteenth-century building.

Proof of the Existence of Saint Eulalia

I've known this settlement since childhood. In the evening the priest's orchard runs out of birds, the sacristan closes the vestry, the light comes up in the presbytery window, and a flock of parish angels come flying to pass the night in the bell tower. The cows returning to the barn greet them with a Gregorian lowing. A sharp fog rises, prickling with mosquitoes.

It's already evening. From now till morning the trains don't stop at the local station, people sleep or drowse, the station shuts down. Only the girls go for walks about the town square, enticing in the radiance of the streetlamps, girls colorful and bulging. Even Jolka at her tender age is strolling about with a pair of apples in her bra, before her real breasts have matured. She accosts me: "Please, please walk with me!"

I can't. I've taken the last train here to see my dying uncle, who has something to tell me. I give Jolka a conciliatory stroke on the breasts; the stems of the apples are turned outwards, they protrude under her blouse, imitating nipples. Jolka purrs at my touch, flutters her eyelids, as if the skins of the pearmains stolen from the priest's orchard were her most sensitive erogenous zone.

I walk off into the darkness, blundering through the mosquitoes like they were thorns. I don't have time to beat them off, I can't be late, my dying uncle, the local parish-priest, has something to tell me. All my life he has had nothing to say to me, evidently he has been putting it off for now.

I am greeted by a weeping muffled by the black kerchief of the priest's housekeeper. The good priest is gone, he went to sleep with the Lord before the evening milking. He's lying in his room, he requested that no one enter. I'm greeted by the curate. The late priest waited, he wanted to share his newest theological discovery with his nephew: proof of the existence of St. Eulalia. Last year he developed proof of the existence of angels; from then on they ran rampant upon the presbytery, domesticated, flaunting their feathers. The jackdaws were even driven from the garrets and chimneys. "In the fight between good and evil, good has triumphed," he would say at that time. Humble was his heart, and fear of the divine stopped him from trying to find proof of the existence of God. He concluded with the angels and began work on the saints, but got only so far as St. Eulalia. Good night.

The din of the bells wakes me like a headache. The angels, woken from the bell tower, fly in a panic over the priest's orchard, pink from sleep and the dawn. They shed feathers in their half-conscious flights. One of them flutters to the gates of the church and, dragging its wings, laps from the basin of holy water; the rest perch on the limbs of the pear and apple trees. That fruit which worms have desecrated from within shakes and tumbles to the ground.

Though I'm thirsty, I won't pick them up. The first train of the morning leaves momentarily. On the platform: Jolka, sleepy and cold. I get aboard, Jolka takes two fragrant and very warm apples from under her shirt and hands them to me for the trip.

I see her getting smaller through the window. She was left alone with wind in her hair, completely flat and child-like, in the unreal colors of the dawn, a cheap picture from the lives of the saints.

The Pink House, or the Desert Sentries

The sand here wasn't just on the surface. Though I sounded at various depths, I only dug up pale yellow, barren sand. And yet, it wasn't as barren as one would be led to believe from its sterile, non-variegated granulation. From time to time, sometimes right below the surface, sometimes deeper, I reached the desert's unique harvest, stone bulbs of considerable dimensions, the firmness of which resided in harmonious contradiction with the soft curvatures of their forms, with their mellow colorings. They were slightly clouded quartzites with limpid interiors; you could peer inside them, into their depths, a bit beneath the surface, and then the pink and inaccessible pulp of the stone started to grow turbid, the

core of its succulence once and for all ripened and became
self-enclosed. Unearthed from the moist depths, they still
glistened for some time with their color of ripening, as if
freshly hatched, only to go gray on the surface soon thereafter, to go blind, to hide themselves under the protective
shell of their suddenly-summoned infirmities. It was, as I
have said, a symptom of the senility of a water-deprived
stone, a testament to its stony vegetation perishing by
drought. The process ran its course most deplorably on
chunks of feldspar, resembling a petrified daybreak. It was
not, however, irreversible. The spar, slightly dewy from
the rain, returned to its proper shape, was restored to the
bold traits of its elemental existence. During the down-
pours its colors intensified to such an extent that, given
one more minute, it could have luxuriantly branched out in
cyclamens or bled raspberry juice.

I tried to dig a hole, but it was hard to climb out with
the stones, so I started scooping out sand from the vertical
walls of the escarpment, boring an ever-deepening cavern.
I carried out the quartzites I had found and laid them on the
dry sand. I wanted to build a pink house, similar at least in
color to the Pink House in which an unforgettable green-
grocer lady with frostbitten cheeks had sold vegetables
over thirty years ago. The scorching heat had whitened the
sand's surface, the unearthed stones aged and withered.
The sandy grotto was already running deep, and my palm
felt the presence of quartzites from the smooth coolness. I

laid my finds in the sun and returned again to the shade of the cavern, because the heat was rising and it had begun to swelter. A few minutes later it started to pour, and now I had a rain shelter. First dust blew around me, rising up from the lashing of the first volleys of rain; a moment later there was the refreshing smell of the sand steaming from the water, and three half-naked men in hooded capes stood at the entrance to my cave.

"We are the desert sentries," said one. With his hands he described a wide circle, as if to indicate the range of the desert space and the extent of his jurisdiction.

"What desert?" I asked in amusement. "Let's not get carried away, gentlemen. You mean this sandbox?"

"We're not about to start explaining things to you," replied the other one.

I stood at the cave entrance. The rain abated, subsided. The desert, however, expanded, the sand stretched to the horizon, perhaps almost to Ostrowia Mazowiecka.*

"Perhaps almost to Ostrowia Mazowiecka," I said in astonishment.

"To what Ostrowia?" shouted the Sentry. "There is no Ostrowia! The desert improves our visibility, so long as it doesn't go to seed, it isn't violated. What are you doing here?"

I wanted to leave; they came up close and blocked my way; I only wanted to show them the stones I had unearthed. I backed up a step. They exchanged whispers and one quickly went off, which seemed to me as mysterious as it was unsettling. Suddenly, the face of one of the two remaining seemed familiar, I latched onto that face until I managed to sort out its provenance. Yes, it was Felek, I mean Feliks, son of a Zaręby pork-butcher, with whom I had once gone butterfly hunting near the train embankments and lured goat-moth caterpillars resembling bloody sirloin from willow trees.

"Hey Felek! Long time no see!" I cried. "Don't you recognize me? It's Jerzy, Jurek. You're looking in good shape! I'm jealous."

He reached out his hand, but it was to gently push me deeper into the cave.

"For now I won't check your papers," he said reassuringly, "I didn't come here for a chat, I'm on duty."

"No horsing around on duty," I added quickly, hoping to salvage some miserable scraps of our friendship, to offer some loyal solidarity.

Sentry Feliks and the other one sat on a pile of quartzites, spat through their teeth, finally the second one again asked:

"What are you doing here? Who's made a mess of this place?"

I started explaining. I only wanted to demonstrate the utter groundlessness of any kind of suspicions or charges yet to be made, which I myself could not have dreamt up. With horror I ascertained that every self-acquitting word sank me deeper and deeper. Sure, I was digging, but I hadn't ruined any crops, and the stones are useless and nobody's property, they're just sitting there, as they did before, except now they are above ground. As I was testifying, the Sentry was writing something with a stick in the wet sand. I was comforted to know that I wasn't just tossing words to the wind, that my words were somehow being officially documented. I therefore spoke slowly and emphatically, repeating some statements twice, in the manner of a dictation.

"And where is it written," I said, enunciating clearly, "that wild field stones are not to be taken? In fact, I know a bit about law: it is not written anywhere. In any case, I haven't taken them. I have only shifted them from place to place. From one place to another. And such a meager distance that in fact nothing has changed. It's just as it was. Even the wind carries things from place to place . . . true, just tiny grains of sand and not these bigger ones, but still. Speaking of the wind, I refer you to sandstorms. They carry things to and fro, and yet the desert remains."

"What have you been doing here?" asked the Sentry for the third time, his stick pausing in its sand notations.

"That's just what I'm telling you. I'd call it the investigations of an amateur mineralogist. If it would do any good I would ask you for a count of the dug-up stones to check if the sums agree with the books. But then I ask: what sums? What books? That's just it; no one has inventoried them, they're not museum pieces. But I assure you, I assure you both, that I have not taken possession of a single piece."

I spoke with vigor, which dehydrated me even more. I had been dehydrated to begin with and now sand was grinding in my teeth. I took a pause in my exposition, because the Sentry on record-taking duty was clearly not keeping up with the minutes. I had already been silent for a bit, and he was still drawing lines in the sand. Suddenly he stared in my direction, inquiringly, it seemed to me.

"Yes," I said. "That would be everything, but I might add that I'm prepared, if necessary, to supply further explanation."

I heard the rattle of a motor approaching, and up drove an open-air buggy, in which rode the third Sentry accompanied by two body-builders. They were olive-brown, clothed in no more than swimming suits, and slathered in oil, their bulging muscles creeping about under their skins like lazy moles. They got out and came towards me with lethargic steps, arms drooping under the burden of inertia. They had the kind of athletic nature that knows no intermediate state between the blow, an eruption of power, and a dormancy that gives the appearance of powerlessness. They stood there, their arms sticking out from their trunks wavering slightly, as though moved by an imperceptible breeze.

"I want to explain . . ." I began.

They interrupted me:

"We know everything."

"This gentleman," I said pointing at the Sentry with the stick, "has officially noted my explanation. Perhaps you would like to familiarize yourselves with it."

They submitted to my request; they both went up to the Sentry, consulted with their heads bent together; he told them something. Sentry Feliks nodded his head as he listened. The stones extinguished one after another, their colors submerged into a stony dusk, while the sun sat at its zenith, once again free from the clouds, the scorching heat packing the body-builders' feet ever deeper in the sand. Only a few quartzite gems, those lying in the shade, teased me with all the juiciness of sliced watermelon. I needed something to drink, and the sight of them, those false promises of satiety, so exasperated my thirst that I got painful cramps.

The council ended. The Desert Sentries and the body-builders approached me. Feliks took the lead.

"Gentlemen," I stammered, "could I request a glass, or a few sips, of water?"

"Don't play games," said Sentry Feliks. "Hear out your sentence in silence!"

"In the name of the Desert," began the choir of body-builders, "in the name of the Desert and with its authorization we convict you to forty-three years of confinement for criminal acts according to paragraphs 7 and 14 of the

Code, for building shelters for the purposes of sowing, and preliminary acts in the interest of fertilization via the removal of stone blockages in regions of future root penetration."

The two body-builders held me tightly, though effortlessly, by the wrists. I didn't try to tear myself free. Sentry Feliks said:

"You have the final word. Go ahead."

"I would like to request," I said, "a few sips of water. I don't want to cause you any trouble, but my throat has gone completely dry . . ."

The body-builders gave Feliks an inquiring glance.

"His throat's gone dry," they repeated.

"That means he won't be able to spit on you," concluded Feliks.

They took me to their car, holding on to both of my hands. Passing by my stones, I saw the inscription that the Sentry had made with his stick in the sand. Was it possible that I had been wrongly convicted? No, there were no words there, nor even letters. On the drying surface of the sand, the drawing, though starting to fade, was still visible: the likeness of a naked woman, voluptuous and spread-legged, much like the portraits seen in tattoos.

Chorzeluk

Unlike Chorzeluk, my great-grandfather Alojzy left something behind. Not that much, but still something. All that remains of Chorzeluk is one photograph taken on Kreszczatik Street in Kiev. He's standing in a long greatcoat, perhaps first year of Gymnasium, casting a shadow and sticking out his tongue. Like a hanged man in time's invisible noose, his tongue lolling out for all of eternity, he survived, bearing testimony to his onetime existence. A false existence? I don't know, I won't draw too many wild conclusions from that tongue.

My great-grandfather didn't pull any unintentionally-everlasting faces, but he did leave a biography. Two episodes from it have survived: one temporal, the other posthumous. As a forest ranger in the Bieszczady Mountains,* on hunts lasting days at a time, he lived off blackberries dug up from under the snow. Right after his death he appeared before my grandmother, silently moving his lips. It was in such a concise description that family tradition passed down the two proofs of the existence of Grandfather, and later Great-grandfather Alojzy, an existence both worldly and otherworldly. Nothing is known of his further adventures; we only know that, with the passage of time, he gained ever-higher rank in the hierarchy of descendants, multiplying the stores of his great-grand-dignity.

Blackberries from under the snow . . . I would like to reach the heart of this episode, reach as far as the taste of those blackberries melting in the mouth, but no sooner do I manage to glimpse the smallest fraction of something, than I see almost nothing at all. The sun reflecting off the Bieszczady snow is blinding in its pure white light. I squint from the painful contraction of my pupils. Great-grandfather Alojzy doesn't even shield his eyes with his hand when staring into the glare beating off the Użocka Pass: his overhanging eyebrows protect him, bushy like a pair of badger tails. Nearby a dog is kicking up a white cloud, digging blackberries from under the snow. It tries to get at the uncovered blackberries with its snowy snout, and jumps back whimpering, its nose stung. Great-grandfather Alojzy chews the fruit slowly. And I pick up a single berry.

It's frozen, hard as a pebble. It melts on my tongue, little by little, and starts to bleed its sour sweetness. Alojzy silences the dog and then I hear that he's crunching frozen blackberries between his teeth like sugar cubes, and is himself listening to the crunching with a rapt attention, paying no notice to the roe deer darting by just a few leagues away. I leave. My feet fall in the heaping snow, I take one more look. Great-grandfather Alojzy is staring at my tracks in the snow, he takes off his rifle.

I returned, shaking last century's snow from my boots. Maybe I'll also try to penetrate the posthumous route to Great-grandfather Alojzy.

He is standing in the circle of light from a large kerosene lamp, cracking his knuckles, and says no more than his silence, emitted from his moving lips. He doesn't suffuse the chill of the grave, but he does smell strongly of rushes, dried in the sun with sweet flag. The smell keeps reminding me of a fish, silently opening its maw on the banks of the San River, the sun reflecting off its scales, dazzling the eyes, a fish pulled from water, as Alojzy was from life.

I listen to the silence, I try to set it into Alojzy's mouth, to formulate it, but all in vain. It was long ago, but I've spent a great many evenings setting words to that scene, and none of the dreamt-up monologues could be questioned, each was a pretender to the singular truth, with pretensions that could not be conquered. But perhaps all the contradictory versions were equally true? Maybe Great-grandfather Alojzy wanted to tell us everything, and for precisely this reason said nothing?

The lamp smokes, the wick sizzles, the ceiling blackens. The grandfathers are silent at the table, parrying Alojzy's silence with their own, underscored by the rustle of the samovar. Great-grandfather Alojzy is tired, he falters on his feet, but he doesn't give in . . . his silence will triumph. The moment will arrive when he leaves the deserted house for good, when he leaves the cold samovar, in the company of the grandfathers . . . to the west, towards Użocka Pass, without leaving a trace behind in the snow.

Unlike Great-grandfather Alojzy, Chorzeluk was unambiguous; no doubt anticipating that the world would take him lightly, he chose not to take the world seriously. And he mocked us, too, we who search in today's old photographs for yesterday, congealed in a past which nobly overstayed its welcome. And maybe he simply stuck out his tongue at that one moment, not imagining the possibility of its perseverance?

I prefer to acknowledge Chorzeluk's ironic intentions, that he, in a manner of speaking, took revenge on his own fate in advance. I must, after all, know something. I cannot forever be straining my ears to hear the silence.

Before the Wall Collapses

G randpa Berberiusz lives in the cellars at number 7. Eyes fixed on his candle, unshaven, with long streaks of gray hair resembling the shoots from cellar potatoes, he greedily listens for news from the outside world, that is, from the blind alley.

The news is invariable. The street has not, since time immemorial, gone on further; it cuts itself off abruptly at a high wall, which obliges it to end right here. But it follows its own course which, when suddenly blocked, veers upward. Not being capable like other streets of happening upon the surface, it attempts to travel by bird-road and mole-road. At its end it piles up towards the high protrusions of chimneys, garrets and turrets. Sometimes I go walking on the turrets and there, at the summit, stomping on the crunchy layers of bird droppings, I look behind the wall, to report the memorized landscape to Berberiusz.

The street, stopped in its tracks, goes underground, where it proliferates into the cellars, crippled and twisted from lack of room. This is where Grandpa Berberiusz lives. It's dark today in his recess, one has to conserve candles, we chat assuming the other's presence.

I tell Berberiusz that it's not only here, it's also up above that the population density is increasing. All the shop signs have become one collective advertisement, on which shoemaker's services are announced beside the Baptist Chapel and the Fine Garments Workshop. That even the birds, for the most part, have their own squatters. That the stress on the wall keeps increasing. Only the Office of Requests and Applications on the first floor has held onto its quite decent living space. I suggest to Berberiusz that he go outside and have a look for himself. I'll help, sometimes one has to burn a bit of candle.

No, Berberiusz won't leave, or even think of going out at this point. Only when the wall collapses. This Berberiuszian waiting, stored up over years, harbors the strength of a revolutionary. The wall is condemned, its days are numbered.

I tell Berberiusz that although the sunrise forces its way through the wall onto our side only at around 10:00, the presence of the wall is by now only partial, less severe than it once was. A wild vine has been planted, the wall is over-grown with its thick verdure and habitude, it has botanized and humanized itself . . .

Berberiusz snorts in the darkness. They want to support the wall? Nothing will help it, though it may be completely clothed in leaves. I nod in agreement. I'll come again, with an exact duplicate of today's news. See you tomorrow, Grandpa Berberiusz.

Berberiusz's grandchildren are sitting in the rectangle of sun at the street entrance. How's everything? He hopes, I say, that it will collapse soon. Ah, says one grandson, he's so sure, he thinks it's a wall, it never gets through to him, though I tell him again and again, that it's the horizon.

Tango Milonga

I have just now woken up, in broad daylight, which is fairly strange. It used to be that Teodora's cries from behind the wall would rouse me at least once during the night. For some days now, I have been awakened by the tense silence anticipating the cry that did not occur. But this time I was finally able to sleep without interruption through the whole period of darkness. I opened my eyes and shut them again. That day was full of motionless light, of glittering perfection, like boiled milk before the skin is lifted. I was afraid to cut into it, lest it stratify into the tumult of earth and the silence of clouds. It was so early, as if the world were just being created.

Just then I heard the Tango Milonga* from behind the

wall, but not the ordinary one, so long-familiar that I had almost no memory of it. This was Teodora's Tango Milonga, exclusively Teodora's, shuffling along like her clothes iron, taming the ironing board for days on end, a tango indulgently garish and sweet, wearing its jujube heart on its sleeve.

I recalled the milonga from its heyday. Once it was piped through the tubes of gramophones. And here it was now, seemingly after the event; the kitchen windows were thrown open and drank in the previously inaccessible spice of life, that tender marjoram, bestowing flavor upon that brief instant between the cleaning of the plates and the dropping off to sleep. Ah! The Tango Milonga, to celebrate every day of the week! At last it became apparent where the stale air was coming from, the air which could not satiate the sighs, where the days of empty waiting were coming from. These days were made to measure for the Tango Milonga, having descended, as prophesied long ago by the Egyptian dreambooks, to fill the space designated for it within the four walls of life.

I heard Teodora's triumphal voice singing along to the gramophone record. And so what if it were a clearance purchase, a tango trampled out on so many dance floors, grown stale from vacant post-carnival halls, from windows surrendering themselves to streets with the flap of a curtain? Even in this degradation, in this apparent capitulation, in time it took up its shady profession as a tear-jerking accomplice to horseradish and onion, a hymn to the local working class.

"Tango of my rev'ries and dreams . . ." crooned Teodora, and let there be no doubt that this was no mere recitation; it was also a confession. Because in fact it was not until recently that Teodora's dreams had had their own melody, true to the rhythm of her breathing, which must be why she had had to cry out in her dreams, her coarse dreams, divested of the virtuosity of whispers and insinuations. But Teodora's waking-time, too, required ennoblement; to this point her only music had been the clatter of doors opening and the lament of the pipes, the shameless noises of the building's digestive system.

I had other music of my own, Teodora's tango was none of my business, but this is telling: from then on picking up my pressed shirts became a solemn occasion, no longer mediocre and meaningless. Entering her room I took off my hat, not as a common gesture of greeting, but as a sign of ecclesiastical worship. Teodora's saliva-moistened finger gave the iron a ritual touch, and I fell silent at the command of the resounding hiss.

I quickly got up and went to collect my shirts. The sight of underwear and starch was a continuum of that morning's whiteness. Teodora continued the day's domestic and colorless activities, the background foundation for all the events yet to be born. These were known in advance to Teodora, she awaited them without anxiety; the tango lifted itself above the spinning record and heralded all the contents of the breaking day, sketching its course in the air, foretelling the day's variable color-scheme till dusk. I repeat: Teodora's tango did not apply to me, and yet I couldn't reject the trust she gave me, initiating me in the Tango Milonga arcana. I resolved to hear everything out without objection, though I had my own entirely different music.

Then I realized to what degree the impersonal tango had assimilated itself to Teodora, become her domestic tango, a tango for every occasion. It filled the gaps in her biography, compensated for the blank spots in her life.

"Haven't you noticed," asked Teodora, "that in films even sadness is more refined, because it's woven with music?"

"I have noticed, but what does the artificial sadness in films have to do with real sadness?" I asked, and was at once ashamed of my question. Teodora wasn't offended:

"And film music? It's artificial too. Only mine is real."

And Teodora replied with that real, absolutely real Tango Milonga, which I render abridged and without any commentary of my own.

"It can be silent," she said, "and yet it's there. All that happens could not exist by itself, without it." For example: Edmund, and his almost daily visits, bringing a nosegay or even a bouquet of roses, mainly tea-roses, because the scent bears a maddening similarity to the melody of the

Tango Milonga. The music plays in tune with the fragrance of the roses, and Ed splits off the thorns with the very long nail on his ring finger so that nothing should wound Teodora. He could do with some caretaking himself, he shouldn't exert himself, he has always been very sensitive, particularly since the time he died in the camps and was buried somewhere in the vicinity of Bremervörde. The flowers on his tin wreath have long since rusted, but he remembers, stops by, and presents live roses, not the slightest bit uglier than the prewar ones. Edmund always seems the same, he hasn't changed one bit, which is a minor miracle to Teodora; he stopped aging some time ago. So he faithfully repeats his old visit, over and over the same visit, presided over by the Tango Milonga. And the words are the same, they are long-familiar, yet always heard for the first time:

"You are heavenly, Teodora," says Edmund, as always, "There is something in you, I swear to God! But what could it be?" Ed asks himself, and replies, "I have no idea, as I live and breathe; there must be an electric current inside you, maybe you heat your iron with the touch of your hand, a hand I will have the pleasure of taking. Before meeting you, let me confide, I lived stupidly, from the bottle to kisses then back to the bottle, till just this very moment, until there was You with that intoxicating tango, something washed over me and I feel like I could be good for you . . ."

Edmund seizes Teodora's trembling hand and presses it to his mouth, his moustache is silken and does not prickle. And Teodora senses that not only has her heart accelerated, but it is blinking red like a traffic light, bathing her again and again in a scarlet flush. When Edmund departs it is easier to be sad to the Tango Milonga, to longingly knit Edmund a scarf. In a free evening, the next one to come along, Teodora jumps out a window to fly for half an hour over Pelcowizna.* "Of course I don't have any wings! But I do have two umbrellas: my own and the one my mother left me. I hook them under my arms and that will carry me, hands free, I can make a scarf on the way. I should somehow repay him for those roses, there were so many of them, isn't that so?" She would have flown during the day as well, but the boys down below are always looking up where they shouldn't. Even if there weren't any wind, the umbrellas would lift her high above the attics, soaring with the sweet breath of the Tango Milonga. It's healthy to go flying sometimes, especially if you can't walk, isn't that so?

No, it isn't: it's evening already! I hadn't even noticed how during Teodora's story the unstained white of day had turned to char, and behind the windows darkness had already come, punctured by the lights of the city. Teodora, propped up on crutches, moved herself towards the gramophone with a laborious scraping, put on a record, lit the lights, turned on the iron, and in a moment had skimmed it with her saliva-moistened finger. I heard a cautionary "pssst," accompanied by the first bars of the tango. I took my package of shirts and got up to leave. With a gesture inviting me to tango, as if to a spread table, Teodora sat down carefully on a stool; she propped her crutches up against a wall. And suddenly, at the moment when I should have said goodbye, I started to dance, or rather . . . it started dancing me.

I try to oppose each note, each bar, to trample them defiantly with small steps or jump forward with carefully-measured and premature leaps, to contradict my unantici-pated unity with the Tango Milonga, under no circumstances to allow the music to synchronize with the stirrings of my body, as independent of me as a fever. I know that for poor Teodora this vainglorious, or so it might appear, demonstration of physical capability might seem awkward. Yet I can't stop. My steps more frequently, ever more frequently, and now without exception, land squarely in the places designated by the melody, become passively obedient, given over to a ritual that is not of my faith, to the rites of a strange cult.

What has become of my staunch principles, my noble autonomy? There is only the Tango Milonga for this moment that never ends, which perhaps has no end, it is a violation to which I surrender, despite the despair welling inside me. And yet that despair gradually stops mattering; it is ready to make any concession, little by little evaporat-ing into a string of melodious sighs, following the demands of the Tango Milonga, Tan-Go-Mi-Loon-Ga! Tan-Go-Of-My-Rev-Ries-And-Dreams! Ta-tii-da-tii-da-tii-da-tidi-da . . .

Shuffle. Slide. Straight ahead. Spin. And back. With the package of shirts pressed tightly to my chest, reeling before the onslaught of the milonga, I danced . . . I don't know for how long. Until the moment when, half-turned, I saw Teodora's hands stretched out towards me and I heard her scream: "Edmund!"

Right then I heard that the record had stopped, but the tango was still there, unfurled in all the corners. I went up to Teodora and kissed her hand. Flushed, with trembling fingers, she disentangled the package of shirts from my hands:

"Ed, how did these roses get so terribly rumpled today?"

"You are heavenly, Teodora. There is something in you . . ."

Window to the World

The unweeded garden of frost has overgrown the window and from behind the thickets of white greenery nothing can be seen. Yet all the same I must stay on the lookout, not lose sight of the world . . . not at any cost. My vigilance, therefore, is in my puffing, keeping open a peephole in the pane, a transparent disc the diameter of my exhalation. For the moment nothing is happening in the world; a dead sky the color of urban snow, etched up with the cawing of crows in sharp leafless charts, and the empty, ever-expectant road. That's all. My breath is hot from impatience, which ensures me a round field of vision, protecting me from leukoma.

What is visible is much like what is not: equally white

and no more variegated than the leaves and flowers of frost. It is the same blinding screen, only pushed further back into the depths, carried over into the landscape, which is also motionless. I don't expect the white to become animated; it's the background upon which my expectations might be fulfilled. For the time being nothing disrupts the whiteness, even my weary breath is white. At times the stiff invariability of the landscape frustrates my hope for change, but the brief passage of a waxwing suffices to make everything seem possible once more. Then I blow doubly, I perfect the difficult transparency, I set my pupils like a trap.

It goes on, it must go on, this I know for certain. And just at that moment of reassurance the stillness is suddenly reanimated; from behind the trunk of an old walnut tree steps Father. With a long beard, for years unshaven, with snow in his hair. In his hand he carries a ball of raffia. Wading through the snowdrifts, he goes from mulch to mulch, parting the straw and grafting some rare varieties of roses onto the shrubbery. He hurries. For lack of time, or is the frost rushing him? His hands are trembling, and the hurry, the feverish hurry immediately spreads to the inoculated stems; the as-yet pale and unripened sprouts show from under the mulchy straw and silently explode at their tips with roses, yellow, pinkening, red. It is that speed, that immediacy which permits both the roses and Father to exist so out of season and out of place. But the moment that the rose settles, after the unfolding of its petals, it falls apart and into the snow. I am so afraid that Father should want to rest! Yet I think he won't, he seems too cautious. He has already left my field of vision, to where I don't know: he returns once more, I can only wish him perseverance. In such frost!

I will be waiting for him . . . here, in the warm kitchen with the murmuring stove. I am protected against cold and against hunger. I have export ham in cans, lard, Cracow groats, potatoes. I can wait like this for a very long time. I will have at last puffed my pane to such a perfect transparency that not only will it no more obstruct my vision, it will become penetrable, like thin air, to let Father in from over there to here, to me, on this side.

I puff and puff, I heat up that circular world before me with the whole capacity of my lungs. The breaths are fainter and fainter, gradually becoming shallow. The white flowers of frost absorb the dusky light, they are yellow, pinkening, red. They go out. The steam from my mouth, instead of salvaging my window to the world, becomes white matter that covers the dying images with vein-ribbed hoarfrost, growing in ever-thicker, glaciated layers.

I am out of breath, Father, I'm no longer able to see, I'm sitting in the warm kitchen, I, your reluctant grave-digger, walling up your tomb with the dead white of January. May the winter treat you gently.

The Sweet Smell of Wild Animals

This was our currency, dating from various mint-
ings, all of which remained in circulation. It was
bought from street kiosks that sold pumpkin
seeds and kvas,* in packs of one hundred, and each one was
made up of five "frames," with holes punched in the sides.
These frames would hold Greta Garbo, and sometimes
even Mickey Mouse or Betty Boop. Incredibly rare, and
thus all the more valuable were the multicolored episodes
from Disney's Silly Symphony; tiny rainbow hatcheries
that molded themselves into the figures of the manifold
idols of entertainment.

The frames of the footage were closed like cages, secur-
ing the motionlessness of their one and only, endlessly

duplicated gesture. They had once opened wide in dark cinemas, setting free all their withheld flutterings, releasing a mutability full of unexpected whims and surprises. It was then that Greta Garbo would release the hand that in my frame was raised to her breast, the hand that could not drop by its own power, and Betty Boop at last gave up her standing posture and, with a lively hoist of her gigantic bosom, went to visit Africa.

That day we left school late after six lessons. In our bags, apart from school accessories, we had what was most important: film, fresh "frames" bought from the kiosk by Zdzienicka's shop. It was not the usual medley, a trek through the cinematic world: these frames were all from one roll of film.

Zoological processions and petrified caravans crossed through them. Camels and elephants made their way forward without so much as a twitch, perhaps the longest and most arduous migration of animals ever, a peregrination pulsing with its potential stomping, seeking no fulfillment, full of imitated poses, movements rooted to the earth.

I located the source of this invasion: the Rialto Theater had just recently stopped running *The Jungle Book*, and no doubt the projectionist had palmed off the parts of the film that had been used up or damaged during the projection, dividing them up into segments. They now recounted the static roaming of animals, told a monotonous tale shorn of its epic proportions, a tale in which nothing happened. I wanted to swap some footage right after I left, but somehow I dawdled and everyone vanished, and I was left in the cloakroom alone. I pulled frame after frame from my pocket and studied them under the light, impatiently urging the animals onwards.

I left quite late. I jumped onto the tram at the last moment, but I couldn't manage to find my ten-ride pass. I eventually pulled out the footage. The conductor yanked it from my hand and punched a hole through the very center.

"I'll buy a ticket, Conductor, sir," I said, "you've made a mistake."

"That will do just fine," he answered with a smile "That will do just fine for this ride."

There was only one other passenger on the tram; his head was bent in sleep and wore a checkered cyclist's cap, his face buried in a shaggy lamb's wool collar. We rode down a street lit up by grocery and fruit shops, their bananas and oranges shining brighter than the occasional neon signs advertising Okocim beer and Majdy's "Revolver" soap. We went faster and faster, until at last I realized that we were racing past all the stops.

"Please, sir!" I yelled to the conductor. "Where are we going? Please stop!"

"Don't yell," the conductor said good-naturedly, pointing at the sleeping man with the cycling cap. "We're coming to the depot."

There was no question of jumping out while the tram

was in motion. It was moving very quickly along some dark, untraveled route that I couldn't identify. At one moment our ride gathered resonance, grew wild with a high, stony undertone; the isolated tumult of the wheels, which until then had been muffled in the vast spaces, now became the focal point of a boisterous polyphony, building a great crash-vaulted clamor rumbling in the dark. The conductor got off, blindly tinkered with something, and the light of a few dozen lamps filled a great red-brick hall with a cement floor. People lying against the walls suddenly awoke and started unwrapping themselves from their colored kerchiefs and rugs. They looked like veterans of some bygone and long-forgotten masquerade, whose music still rang in their bones. Despite their drowsiness, they lifted themselves up from their lairs in a complaisant, ambling rhythm, unwinding and winding their peacock colors as the music dictated. The air smelled sickeningly sweet, the odor of withering, or rather dead flowers.

The conductor returned to the tramcar and delicately shook the sleeping passenger:

"Master, don't sleep master, we're here."

The checkered cyclist's cap lifted itself and I saw the face, the mock-comic face with its tragic eyebrows drawn high on the forehead, its nose as vermilion as a pimento, with the stock smile of a clown. He rubbed his dark green eyelids with his palms, after which he proudly displayed his clean, unsullied hands to the conductor.

"It doesn't come off," he said. "It doesn't come off. It's already soaked into my blood. Let's go, Ripoletti!" he said, addressing me.

At first I thought he was speaking to someone behind me; I looked around, there was no one.

"Yes, Ripoletti, I'm talking to you," he said.

We both got out and right away the hall's residents started entering the empty tramcar with their bundles and rugs, to settle immediately into another sleep. We crossed through the hall, which was silent, except for the patter of the whirling cockchafers in the enameled lampshades. By the opposite, shadowy wall stood camels and elephants, as if penned in by the walls improvised from old wardrobes, cupboards and ottomans. One ottoman, its plush beet-red upholstery torn away, stripped of its sedge, revealed almost naked springs. No doubt fodder for the starved animals. They now stood motionless with half-gaping jaws, and the sweet fragrance grew in intensity as we approached them.

"Take this, Ripoletti," said the Clown, giving me two buckets. "We've had a long, a very long standstill. The elephants have succumbed to corrosion, they need a total overhaul; and we'll need to get rid of the camels entirely."

I went up to the motionless menagerie. Indeed: the elephants were in urgent need of repair. There were deep caverns in their sides, at the base of their legs, and also around the knees: dark hollows emitting radial lines of cracks. The decay was very advanced, there was no time to lose, the elephants had to be mended, they could hardly stand with such serious damage; imagine what might happen when they danced to the circus waltzes! A careless prance might tear the animal in two, splitting the healthy parts of its body.

The Clown brought me a bucket of wet cement, the elephant lifted the bucket with its trunk, and I started patching up the holes, filling them with a shovel. The cavities were so vast they seemed bottomless. The Clown kept bringing the brimming pails, which proved barely enough for two fillings: under the knee of a hind leg, and in the stomach. When he went for the next load of cement, a girl furtively came out of hiding from behind a camel, a girl whom the light revealed to be in fact a very skinny dwarf.

"Please, Mr. Piroletti . . ." she said softly, in a slightly croaking voice, "I left something there."

"Ripoletti, Ripoletti, if you please," I corrected her, as if in total agreement with that strange name I had received by mistake, taking care that it not be mispronounced. Her formal address seemed perfectly natural: she was, after all, so tiny.

"Excuse me, Mr. Ripoletti," she whispered. "Could you give me some help? I left behind something important."

"Where?"

"In the elephant."

With her little hand she indicated towards a hole in a

front leg that I had not yet touched. I found a spotted compact and gave it to the little woman.

"Thank you," she squeaked, curtseying low, "those are all my savings, I hide them from the Clown, he takes everything away, and I've got to be putting something aside for the future. Because, just between us, could a rational person believe that these elephants will ever move?"

How could I know if there was any chance for success? I was only instructed to fill in the holes, the rest wasn't up to me. Nor was the fate of the little woman any of my concern, I shouldn't have bothered my head over it. And yet . . .

"Listen," I said, suddenly baffled by her minuteness, "Listen to me. I'm leaving here, it's dark, no one will catch me outside the depot. You can come with me."

"Where to?" She asked, terror in her eyes.

"Away, just away from here. You have savings, you can mend tights. Do you know how to fix a ladder?"

"Thank you, Mr. Ripoletti. I'm not leaving here. I know that nothing's going to come of all this, but I've been sitting here for sixty-seven years and two months. Quite a while, huh?"

I took the footage from my pocket, my journey of camels and elephants to nowhere.

"Please take this. It'll do just fine," I said, unintentionally echoing the conductor's phrase, "It'll do just fine."

She looked at one frame under the light and nodded.

A nocturnal chill blew in from the open gates of the depot. She covered her withered face and, without saying farewell, departed into the depths of the hall, greedily inhaling the sweet smell of wild animals.

An Escape

We started digging three months ago. It would have gone more quickly if we hadn't had to keep the utmost vigilance. We dug up the earth a bit at a time and scattered it in various corners of the camp, the tunnel slowly increased in length, and we, initially impatient and excited, grew to have a taste for this mole-like work, as if it weren't the road to freedom but freedom itself, sparingly dosed out, without excessive risk. The darkness of the underground corridor was as quiet as the womb; it already seemed remote from the carbolic acid and rutabaga smell of the camp air, though it was still far from the incommensurable space beyond. I knew, and perhaps Michał felt the same, that nothing bad could happen to us there, that the soil itself conspired with us in our silent struggle towards the surface, as it aids the germination of seeds. I knew that we could trust it.

Today was Michał's turn; we met in the evening at the barracks. He was cutting the potato he had stolen from the kitchen into slices and baking it on the iron pipe of the furnace; he had connections, knew the camp like the back of his hand, he said: "We'll make it to the end, brother. Just a few more meters." "That won't be too short?" I asked. "Wouldn't it be better to carry on a bit further?"

"Further?" Michał bridled. "And do you know what's further on? They say there's another branch of the camp!"

I didn't want to quarrel with him, but why should we hit the other branch? Tomorrow it'd be me. Fine, I'll pull up, towards the way out. But . . . to what way out exactly? Burrowing in the earth for months, plunged in darkness, in the one bit of labor done out of our own free will in years, we hadn't given any thought to the next phase, the foreign terrain, the wilderness of freedom, which wasn't necessarily on our side. Before falling asleep, lying in my bunk, I thought about those remaining few meters. As long as our burrowing continued, still far from the daylight at the end of the tunnel, it seemed to me that our captivity would end together with the arrival of that light, and so our labor and unrest was confined to digging, scraping, tunneling. Now with my eyes closed, at the very bottom of the darkness, that bright opening appeared, and the corridor took off into the unknown, into a light which less illuminates than blinds.

My hands groped in the darkness for a nail pounded into the planks over the headboard, for trustily hidden reserves from the morning, a cigarette butt and matches. I had never been good at arranging amenities for myself, but for so many years I had had to make do somehow. The match flame momentarily revealed the whole wretched setup: the warm blanket made of the poplar down I had collected, which turned out to be no worse than cotton; a cup made from a can with a makeshift handle; some old newspaper to use for rolling cigarettes, as well as a very mutilated book: more or less three quarters of *The Spirit of the Forest*. Not much, and it had to be left behind. I greedily sucked up the smoke and the nocturnal coziness of my corner, shut away from the wind and the screams of the guards. The plume of smoke, illuminated by my cigarette, hung over me as gently as a cloud.

I decided to have a talk with Michał; up till that point we had spoken only about the tunnel, and it was high time we thought about the next stage, which I was trying in vain to imagine. At the morning assembly I pulled him aside and immediately became convinced that the same thing was tormenting him. It was dark out, not yet dawn. There was a long silence before Michał confessed he had an idea. In the camp latrine, which we called the "collective," due to the lack of partitions, he shared his plan with me. "We would get snagged," he said, "from the very start: it's foreign terrain, who knows where the roads are and where they lead to, we'll freeze up; that kind of freedom cages you more than the barbed wire, you can't move a muscle. We won't make it without a guide, but, fortunately, we might have a guide. He'll instruct us. Give us pointers."

This was an old, paralyzed sapper, Major Pietrasiak, long ago crossed off of the camp files. So as not to have him taken to the infirmary, or the "deathery" as we called it, a group of friends hid him, somehow concealing him day by day in a crawlspace under a bunk. Taking advantage of a delousing operation, we looked in on Major Pietrasiak, and, squatting, set forth our proposal: as he was known for being familiar with the area, he would point to and sketch out the escape route, so that we wouldn't be entirely in the dark. I told him carefully about our preparations and about the tunnel. Would the Major agree, and . . . for how much?

The Major's face bolstered my confidence. I can only assume that this was because of his moustache: it was gray and spread across his bloodshot, apoplectic face, it bewinged that face, lifting it aloft and bestowing it symmetry. Of course, I realized, the white eagle, the white eagle! He didn't respond right away, he considered things in silence, until a cigarette held out by Michał loosened his lips: Well, he's not surprised that we've come to him. As a guide, a reconnaissant even, there's no question, the situation is plain and simple, and his services in this department, back under the tsar, were acknowledged by a special order and badge from the Outdoorsmen's Society. All the same, it was hard for him from there, from under the bunk, to say everything from a distance, in advance. "Leadership," he said, "is above all flair and empiricism. Allow me to sign aboard, as the third party, and I'll lead. Above all: empiricism. That's my motto."

As if on command, we simultaneously glanced at the Major's powerless legs.

"So what then?" he answered our glances, "You'll pull me through the tunnel, and then carry me by turns . . . But not a word to anyone. Lips sealed."

All we were missing was the command: Dismissed! It seemed to me there was not only a note of caution in the old man's voice, but also some sort of threat. I tried to explain to myself that this only resulted from the difference in rank between him, a major, and us, a corporal and a sergeant, but at the same time I already knew that the deal was closed; Pietrasiak was initiated and there was no turning back. From that moment to the completion of the tunnel, the Major summoned us under various pretexts a few times daily. We came running together or in turns, once Michał, once me, even if just for a moment, knowing that otherwise, seized by suspicions, he would have trumpeted our intentions to the whole of the camp. I started to fear the Major, but Michał reassured me: We can't make it without him, and he depends on us, he wouldn't get anywhere by turning us in. Maybe this was true. My original enthusiasm for the Major had vanished, though, without a trace. How could I ever have associated that nicotine-yellowed clump of moustache with the eagle? That's how far you can be deluded by appearances! Had camp life warped my imagination to such an extent?

Forget it, not important. The last hours were the worst. For the first time, I didn't touch my soup. I couldn't: my imagination was yoked to intensive training for the escape; I had already visualized myself in the subterranean passage while lying on the bunk, palms soaked in sweat. Just before the barracks were closed we lugged Major Pietrasiak into the bushes behind the latrine, and later, under the floorboards of our own barracks, into a hatchway. The guard came, counted us, and locked the door as he left, and then Michał moved first, pulling the tightly-clinging Major behind him, and I pushed Pietrasiak's powerless legs from the rear. We crawled on our stomachs, the Major half supine. From time to time he gave instructions: "Onwards, keep moving, straight ahead!" as if any other direction were possible.

"Major," whispered Michał breathlessly, "you can give directions as soon as we get to the surface, OK?"

"No," replied Pietrasiak with dignity, "I took full responsibility for you two from the very beginning!"

Michał didn't respond, and I secretly thanked him for this. I didn't want to risk displeasing the Major in any way, let him speak; and so from then on we took his identical-sounding instructions in panting silence.

There was no sun dawning at the mouth of the corridor, no blinding streaks of light such as those I saw behind my closed eyes before falling asleep. The approaching end of our underground crawling was marked only by the chilly smell of the air, much like the night before, when I had reached the end of the tunnel for the first time, tossing aside the last handfuls of earth. Now, although we could feel a refreshing draft, we moved very slowly: Pietrasiak was plenty heavy, and most of the weight was centered in his legs, which were neutral, so to speak, taking no part in the escape.

We came out in the middle of the night, which would have been moonlit had it not been for the clouds. We hauled Pietrasiak a few dozen meters more along the ground, and then we fell at his side, panting for breath.

"Major, now it's your turn," I said. But Pietrasiak gave no response, totally consumed by his breathing. So again I said, "Major, there's not a second to lose!"

"Indeed, indeed," he muttered, sitting on the grass. "Above all, we have to establish our directions. That's a basic affair, the foundation of empiricism . . ."

"So go ahead and establish them, then," groaned Michał impatiently.

Pietrasiak swept his gaze all about, aided by the moon, which peeked out for a moment. He stretched out his neck, putting his face forward; he sniffed the air.

"If we turn our faces southward," he began at last, "on our left we will have the east, and on our right . . . the west . . . I need not add that we will have the north behind us . . ."

I was able to stop Michał's fist at the last moment: "What's with you? Leave him alone! This is a sick old man. Let him finish. We are listening, Major."

"The question remains: which way is south?" the Major continued. "We have to look for a tree. A tree, you know, trunks are covered in moss on the southern side . . ."

I felt I would not be able to pacify Michał. A dark, totally treeless plain stretched to the very horizon. The one tree in this vicinity was the ash tree inside the camp, next to the guard house.

"Why did we take him with us?" snorted Michał. "Major Ballast! Major Ballast! Soon you'll be covered in moss yourself."

"I'm going back," I stammered, "Michał, let's go back."

"Take me with you!" screamed Pietrasiak, "You won't just leave me behind!"

"You wanted freedom, well you've got it." Michał tore himself from the grass.

Major Pietrasiak grabbed him with both hands and in the blink of an eye was hanging off his shoulders: he groaned "Can't take a joke, friends? Can't take a joke?"

"Shake him off!" I cried to Michał, "Shake him off and quick back to the tunnel!"

Michał struggled, tried to get loose, but all for nothing. It was as if all the strength that had abandoned Pietrasiak's legs had resettled in his arms and hands. He didn't let go, clinging to Michał's back as tightly as a hump.

"Now straight ahead," ordered the Major. "That'll be north-northwest. After two kilometers, I'll tell you when, we'll make an adjustment to the west; now we'll pass the swamp, about six hectares of swamp. Forward!"

"Michał!" I cried, "He's lying, don't believe him!"

But Michał was already going at full trot in the direction indicated by Pietrasiak, with the Major's face like a standard waving over his head. I could still hear the pit-a-pat from inside the tunnel as I crawled feverishly so as to reach my bunk before roll call, before somebody noticed my absence.

Mimesis

"**D**o you know what it means to retreat into seeming non-existence in order to exist? To annihilate yourself in other people's eyes in order to survive? If you were, begging your pardon, a cockchafer, a grasshopper, a lizard, you would know all this, and you would know nothing. Yet *they* have made no sacrifice; they've already adjusted, they were born as apparent blades of grass, would-be leaves, supposed stones. Only movement could betray them, but movement is their escape. And what if there is no escape, if you should be, do forgive me, as estranged from yourself as we are?"

These words rang out in the old cluttered woodshed. Despite the closed door it's fairly bright in here: plenty of light, shaded green by the lilac bushes, seeps in through the gaps and knotholes. There's no draft, but I've noticed that the sheets of cobwebs near the thick purlin high above are billowing, as though catching the words spoken. I realized that the purlin was speaking to me, though in fact it wasn't a purlin, but rather someone who in a bid to survive had concealed himself not behind something, but *as* something, taking shelter in the thing itself, assuming its exterior.

I made no response. These very confessions were a partial unmasking, a momentary disclosure; my reply could urge them on, thwart such a powerful will to vanish. I won't respond. Let's say that there was silence, a silence that required neither opposition nor confirmation, but which could be either respected or broken. The logs clattered as I threw them into the corner, I was determined to wait this out, even if it had to speak once more.

I won't say a thing. We had once been friends, after all, and now Izydor didn't know me; could I have changed too? Now I understand his rapture at having lost all resemblance to himself. I can imagine his new concerns: fire and bark beetles. I know: he has gone and hidden so well that he'll never find himself now. I remember how he burrowed in the woodshed attic years back, bound to it by his fear, but still himself.

What desperate will to live drove you, Izydor, into the cocked hat of this purlin? The similarity is becoming your identity, the outer coat of paint is seeping into your depths, it is becoming your substance. You can't stay intact without making an escape, even in this altered shape. You got carried away, Izydor, you definitely got carried away.

That's all I would have had to tell him, that is, if I had wanted to speak. That would have been my reply to his attempts to excuse himself, to his arguments murmured in groaning whispers. I threw the last log in the corner. My work was finished for the day. In the still of the woodshed, that same monotonous groaning drew itself out, but now without any words, an unarticulated condemnation, though as profound as despair.

It was a wasp's nest as big as a human head, a sphere of paper maché protruding from the ceiling, in the corner, in the shadow of the purlin, full of buzzing caprice. In the pool of light I see hundreds of circling insects, picking at the wood of the old purlin with their mandibles and building pale red galleries and fortresses onto their palace. Yellow zigzags fly closer and closer to me with a buzz of impatience. My instinct smells danger. Time to escape the woodshed.

An Attempt at a Dialogue

She was supposed to be sitting by the first window in the Miedzianka Café, one of those metropolitan cafés that still smells of wet paint and has no identity of its own. I arrived punctually, but the table by the window was empty. Ordering a small coffee, I whiled away the time with some calligraphy; on a napkin I wrote out the letters of her surname with decorative flourishes. Firanelli, Firanelli, FIRANELLI. I didn't know the owner of the name personally, I didn't even know her first name: she was my good non-acquaintance, a dream companion older than her years. Ages before I learned about Leoncavallo or Verdi, I had already gotten to know three Italian citizens of my town: Lardelli the cake-maker,

Franboli the confectioner, and Firanelli the electrician. Only the last did I have the opportunity to meet personally, the others I knew from shop signboards and labels. These shops and sweets no longer exist, Firanelli died long ago, and the last reminders of Milan or Florence survive in the occasional Italian ice-cream shop.

It's been years since I lived in my hometown; I've come especially to meet the daughter of the late Firanelli, and I'm staying in a hotel. I woke up early and couldn't get back to sleep, excited by the conversation in store for me. I walked the streets aimlessly, twice getting lost, and the second time I was too embarrassed to ask for directions; I hailed a taxi and went to the Miedzianka. At that time of day it was empty, there were only a few pensioners dozing over their newspapers. It was good that we had arranged a certain table because, having never met before, she could have mistaken me for one of those old men. Strange as it may sound, I had in fact not arranged to meet here with Miss Firanelli, but with an extension of her father, with a living opportunity to confirm my memories. It now seems symptomatic that I never wondered what she would look like, though I found myself casting an eye at the dark-haired girls entering the café: I hoped to recognize her by her complexion. All the black-haired women looked around uncertainly and then sat at other tables. Some flickering fluorescent lights were on, and all the faces went blue in the glow; all of them, that is, except for the one which was bent over me.

Miss Firanelli had been standing there silently for a good minute before I noticed her. I had supposed that someone had switched on a lamp nearby, a lamp with a shade. She had long, very fair hair that fell onto her shoulders in straight strands. We sat down. While waiting for the waitress I decided to state at once the reason for having bothered her to come. I said:

"It was hard for me to explain myself over the telephone. Perhaps you'll forgive me . . . I knew your father and I would like to talk about him. I promise that this is a subject as near to me as it is to you. I don't think you could imagine how much your father has meant to my life, though to an outsider it might seem that Mr. Firanelli only came in contact with my home, that is, the home of my family, in the capacity of electrical installation work. This may be true, but so what? He still had an impact on my life, and my dreams in particular. I'll tell you as much as I can, and perhaps you'll be kind enough to tell me what I don't know, because I'd like to know everything."

Miss Firanelli smiled gently and took to nibbling one of her fingertips, as if she wanted to keep her smile from becoming a grin, and her teeth slowly slid back from the slope of her nail. The waitress arrived with a menu. Miss Firanelli, her smile fading, looked at me with motionless eyes and fluttering eyelashes, as if she wanted to tickle me with them till I smiled.

"What would you like to order?" I asked her. She

picked up the menu, and placed it in the center of the table, leaning over it like it was a pool of water. Her breasts peeked out from behind her loosely-hanging blouse; they were as round as oranges, and stood on their nipples, now flattening, now rounding out, to the rhythm of a few consecutive breaths.

"The house beverage and mocha cake!" And returning to me, she said "That is interesting indeed. Please go on."

And so I went on:

"At this point you should know that I was then five years old, and I was very afraid of the dark. At night, after the lights went out in my bedroom, there was only an impenetrable blackness; my fear caused it to gradually grow pale, to fill itself up with whirling patches of whiteness, an emanation of my terror. And then those scraps of fictitious half-light began to swell, rushing into my dreams in a black-and-white panic, hastily organizing themselves into figures and events that I had to take part in. Because my dreams, to that day, had been only black-and-white. And it was your father . . ."

Miss Firanelli crossed one leg over the other, revealing one to halfway up its garter, which, stretched to its limits, appeared to be only just restraining that uncommonly long leg from growing further. That sudden change in the position of Miss Firanelli's legs threw me off. This gesture revealed her entire self-sufficiency: it was a gesture whereby Miss Firanelli embraced Miss Firanelli. She is perhaps so saturated in herself, I thought, that my pointless words aren't getting through to her. Suddenly, I heard:

"And so? And it was my father, it was my father . . ."

And yet she had heard.

"And it was your father who changed everything. His appearance marked the start of my dreams in full color. It went like this: One afternoon my father brought in your father. That was when I saw him for the first and last time. He pulled gold and silver wires out from an enormous bag, and I quickly realized that this was a trap for the nocturnal birds of my dreams, a snare for the dark beasts that came running every night into my room, as if returning to their lairs. Your father smiled comprehendingly at me, and I was grateful to him, although I still didn't know everything. I'm sure you remember that knowing smile, that smile behind which his eyes remained serious and slightly sad . . ."

Miss Firanelli started to speak. Her words, though on the surface not devoid of meaning and proper semantics, were in fact unarticulated. Like oranges cultivated through centuries of pomological procedures into mere pulp, deseeded to give nothing but flavor, a blind plunge into juiciness, such were her words, no longer meaningful, drawing their compelling strength solely from their sound. I tried in vain to defend my truths, the incorporeal algebra of my reasoning, none of which seemed to deserve her approval. I claimed no right to her solidarity. I only counted on an alliance out of regard for her father, in memory of him. I was not overrating the value of my reminiscences, but I realized that this was the victory of tangible things over illusory ones, the triumph of the apple over Newton. Anyway, I wouldn't say that Miss Firanelli stood against me: she was only adjacent, always outside of everything that I came to her with. I found that the tiniest curl of her lips into a grimace, the slightest dawning of an ear from amidst her hair smothered even my most impetuous words with its relentless silence. I found that my confidences became, like it or not, ceremonies in praise of Miss Firanelli.

"Were they like mine? Is it true they were the same?" she asked.

"What?"

"My father's eyes."

I gave her a sideways glance. There wasn't much similarity. Her pupils dilated suddenly, full, it seemed, of some gnawing hunger, like a quarry pulling me to its black spaces within. No, Miss Firanelli is not the light around which I shall spin, I decided to defend myself. I assured her:

"I was only five then, no more. I was tortured by dreams. And your father's smile, oh I don't know, maybe it was similar to yours, it gave me hope. My room was on the second floor, with a window onto the garden, but at night all the windows looked out onto the night. It had already started to grow dark when your father finished all his work. On that night, for the first time a small red light shone from the ceiling, and just imagine, my dreams turned scarlet; the following day, under a green light, my dreams were like a leaf swollen with chlorophyl; another time they had an indigo prologue thanks to a blue lamp . . . Sometimes your father popped into my dreams for an inspection, I came across him in various dreamscapes, in zones of various colors, as he checked that everything was running smoothly, staving off short circuits, which sometimes, in his absence, snuffed out the colors in a single flash and catapulted me and my scream into reality. But with your father, that never once happened. I could tell you more about our meetings, but I never again saw him during the day. You knew your father from a different, I would say, more down-to-earth perspective."

"Yes. Maybe we could get out of here; better to talk in the open air. All riiight?"

The first part of that "right" was in itself an autonomous question, full of fear and helplessness. The second part served as a response, which permitted no contradiction and had the spark of an amiable threat. Miss Firanelli got up, and I quickly leapt to my feet, so as to pick her gloves up from the floor. But it was only the sudden movement of the shadow she cast behind her as she stood. I withdrew a step, startled by my misplaced gesture, and we left. It was cloudy and gray. Miss Firanelli led the way; her step was confident, totally sure that the correct route would fall under her feet. I trusted my companion, this town had become foreign to me, and anyway I had no sense of direction; I got lost wherever I went. I had to admit that I envied her confidence; I was always stumbling about on the edges of an awkward world, but nothing blocked her path, things shifted out of her way like a set on a revolving stage.

I trusted blindly in where our stroll was taking us, it was outside of my control. It didn't matter, even the hope of building an understanding with Miss Firanelli had abandoned me. I gave her my arm, and it might have seemed that I was leading her. The street we went down was a totally new thoroughfare, I couldn't recall ever having seen it before. I was attached to this town, my home of years gone by, but nothing I saw seemed to confirm this attachment, and of the past events that I did recall, none could be tailored to fit a single concrete place, or traced back to their rational origins. The buildings, too lofty and ornamented with lifeless façades, were already covered in multicolored tangles of neon. Yet they had nothing of my dream palette, no Firanelliesque colors to lull me to sleep. This was the throbbing pulse of metropolitan life.

"When my father was alive," said Miss Firanelli all of a sudden, "neon had already appeared, but he didn't know much about it. Do you know that your light bulbs must have been painted on the outside?"

"I know, and with time the paint on them cracked, and then started to peel, letting out ordinary light in places.

But when they were new, I tell you, neon like that doesn't exist."

She nodded. She showed neither the inclination to argue nor to agree. What could she care about this light or that, she gave off her own radiance; it was not by accident that I had at first taken her for a lamp with a warm shade. But now I knew for sure that there was no relationship between myself, the enchanted, and her, the daughter, that from so far away Master Firanelli could not manage to unite us in anything. Miss Firanelli had nothing to offer but herself, she was entirely harnessed to her self-promotion. I wanted to satisfy that desire, repay her for her trouble with a word concerning her. I said a few such words, then a few dozen, I said much more than I intended to. I felt my truths begin to falter and yet, renegade, I pressed on towards her, to submit to the dictates of the beauty spot over the left corner of her mouth. I began to despise myself, but even this contempt raised her to new heights: I would say the high heels of her shoes were forged of that contempt. She clicked them rhythmically, she carried herself with nimble steps and walked with poise, even in the darkest of streets she lit her way with a smile. I was already close to dismissing both Firanelli and his electrical constellations to merely gain her approval, when Miss Firanelli stopped:

"There's something in my shoe," she said, standing on one leg and balancing herself against me, throwing her arm around my neck . . . and she shook the invisible pebble from her shoe. Her hair tickled me, and I couldn't even scratch myself. I felt angry, blaming myself and not her for that embrace. I attempted a retreat, I struggled to fix my mistake, I explained that her fingernails reminded me of my red lamp, and thus the unintentional digressions, the associations built around her . . .

"You see, I couldn't show what I was talking about, so I demonstrated it somehow on you, to make everything as it were, visible: the green lamp on your skirt, the red on your fingernails, the blue in your eyes. Because, after all, it's been so long since I had those lamps . . ."

I paused, seeing that I wasn't fixing anything with this stumbling explanation, that I was only spoiling all that remained, and irreversibly. She pouted her lips and said:

"I don't have any either. Father didn't even live to his retirement, all those things got sold long ago. I can't do anything for you."

I didn't even feel bad, her suddenly officious tone didn't startle me. I had had enough of Miss Firanelli, I had had enough of myself. Of the idiotic confessions of incommunicable matters. What exactly did I want from her, what did I hope to gain? I had had enough, and I would have immediately said farewell and departed, were it not for the fact that we were in a strange part of town at night; I couldn't leave her just anywhere, and besides, I could get lost myself, I would get lost without Miss Firanelli. We walked on together in complete silence. I passed lamppost after lamppost, two shadows ran opposite us, as though they sought to bring us together, and then, repelled, they fled behind us. I hadn't the faintest idea why despite everything Miss Firanelli kept walking beside me, when she could have run off. We were no longer bound by either my tri-colored illusions or Miss Firanelli's faith in her power over me. We were no less strangers than before we met at the Miedzianka.

I wasn't paying any attention to the darkening streets slipping past, until in the circle of light from a lamp I noticed a pink hawthorn bush in blossom. Where had I seen that hawthorn, that pink hawthorn? I lifted my head: the lamppost, too, was long-familiar, topped with what looked like the head of a bird with a bad case of the Secession. Miss Firanelli silently pushed the half-open gate and pulled me by the hand. We went a few dozen steps through the dark smell of some kind of flowers, whose name I've forgotten. When she opened the door of the house, I recognized it. Filtrowa Street, number 47! I went up the oak stairs in the dark, by memory: It was entirely my legs' memory, taking each stair with confidence, knowing the height and count of each one, I didn't have to hold the railing. Miss Firanelli went in front of me. And so I was there once again, where I could never have come alone, if not for her, who had led me! And I had suspected her of betraying her father!

Through the door left ajar to the corridor a beam of

greenish light fell on Miss Firanelli.

"Miss," I began, full of gratitude and a troubled conscience. She cut me off, ordering silence with a finger to her lips. We slipped softly into the room. Master Firanelli's green light glowed from the ceiling. My childhood crib by the wall was empty; the pillow was crumpled, the blankets tossed about. I went up to it: the sheets were still warm, warmer than the palm of my hand. Where could I have gone at such a late hour, after just having woken up? Miss Firanelli joined me at the empty crib and lay down; it was much too small for her, and her legs rested on the high horizontal bars; she didn't let go of my hands for a moment, and now she pulled me towards her. Not here! Not here! I thought ruefully, but these thoughts, like alarm signals, receded ever further into the distance, until finally they were inaudible. I plunged my hand into Miss Firanelli's hair and felt my fingers sting with a swarm of sparks. She smiled, revealing her wet green teeth. I put out the smile with my lips.

And just at that moment I heard a little pitter-patter coming nearer from behind the door. I was coming back! We had to leave. I pulled Miss Firanelli with all my might and brought her up against a wall, between a wardrobe and the door leading to the hallway. She brushed her hair away from her face and stared at me with what might have been hatred. I ordered her to be silent, not with a finger, but with my whole hand covering her mouth. The door creaked and in I came, tiny even for a five-year-old, bare-foot, with a shirt down to my ankles. I slipped under the covers, and from there I stared in our direction with eyes squinty from yawning. Sideways, sideways, along the wall, then we darted through the door and slid down the stair-case railing without so much as a rustle.

On the street, Miss Firanelli walked quickly in front, and when I had closed the gate behind me she had already gained a significant lead. I tried to hurry my steps, but she just did the same. I couldn't shout out, because how? I didn't know her name. The moment she vanished around the corner of a building at the end of the street, I realized that I was passing the entrance to my own hotel. I took a good look at the spot where Miss Firanelli had vanished, but it was completely empty. She had taken it to heart, too bad. Maybe she would return later?

In the hotel room, I lay down at once, but sleep wouldn't come. As I always do in times of insomnia, I summoned up the memory of an old dream, replaying parts of it before my open eyes. Normally, this was a dream memorized and reshaped by numerous recollections, meant to serve as a decoy for sleep, which was biding its time before arrival. But this time it was a childhood dream, one long-forgotten and from decades past. I recalled it suddenly and precisely:

I was lying in bed on the second floor, a green dream light surrounding me, and I saw two people by the door in the corner of the room, a woman and a man, staring at me as my parents sometimes would, making sure that I was sleeping peacefully. But these weren't my parents; these strangers were afraid of me, I saw it in their eyes. I didn't have to be afraid any more. I had triumphed in silence over their fear, and though they quickly bolted into the corridor, edging sideways along the wall to the door left ajar, they weren't long outside my field of vision, because soon I was sailing my pirate vessel across a great green space, an ocean as deep as my dreams, with those two tied up, captive, strapped to a mast flying a black flag . . .

Through my hotel window, you could still hear the rumble of some nighttime buses, and I'm not sure when that black hotel sleep finally overwhelmed me, a sleep without dreams or apparitions. When I got dressed the following day, I had quite a bit of time left before my train departed. I went towards the building around which Miss Firanelli had disappeared. She hadn't gotten far: I found her right around the corner! She fit quite perfectly in the two dimensions allotted her on a large and colorful board decorating a coffee shop display. Smiling at the inscription: DRINK SULTAN COFFEE, her hand held a cup filled with dark liquid, spiritualized by a spiral of steam. She celebrated her new mission on that poster, rendering to Sultan Coffee all the favors that had theretofore served only herself. The smile, accustomed to the exclusive promotion of its bearer, opted for Sultan Coffee; the narrowed eyes, with which Miss Firanelli held sway over myself and the world, became a point in favor of Sultan Coffee; the slightly distended nostrils invited passersby to Sultan Coffee as though to a kiss.

I had never suspected she would cease to be self-sufficient, that she would lend her aura to coffee. Yesterday I still thought she would return, to continue her primeval rite of selfhood before me, but in vain. Now she stared motionlessly at me through her eyelashes; with that coffee cup held in her two slender fingers, halfway between the saucer and her lips, she could simulate her voluptuousness even in the two dimensions of the color billboard. All at once, I felt my mouth start to water. Swallowing back a few times, I went in and asked for a large coffee.

The Joy of Dead Things

I continue down the street, which becomes less than a street, because as it gets further from the train station the pavement thins, grass sprouts out, the street grows wild. Its dwarfish houses are in decline, the undeveloped spots between them empty, with an afterwards emptiness, the result of an annihilation, like gaps between an old man's teeth.

This place is no longer good for living, it's for roosting. The single House that has survived, that one on the right, the sole one amidst the collapsing hovels, is tall and vacant, with dark holes instead of windows. Birds fly through them from end to end like through the autumn crowns of poplars; the House more resembles a tree than the nearby huts.

The shacks appear with less and less frequency, and I still can't find the diner where I once left my last twenty złotys. Maybe they're still there on that faience plate beneath the window. I want to find the diner, but I have to go quickly, so onwards.

Because: I am moving to the rhythm of my heart, precisely, as if on command; I cannot fall behind it. I breathe more and more quickly from fatigue, keeping track of my pulse, which goes faster and faster, by placing a hand on my heart. And I speed up, I have to keep pace, my tired heart again gets ahead, I give chase, now I'm running, I can't break the tempo, mustn't part with myself. I run as breathless as a drum major who has lost control of his beat, a mutinous, dictatorial beat. Its racing patter from within my ribs and the shallow breaths, this is the melody of the march.

I'm running. I can't find the diner. I see other shops with rusted signboards whose letters have become illegible. Closed shops. You could get into them through their low, smashed windows, but then there's nothing inside them anymore. I still have a few handfuls of coins. They're weighing me down as I run, there's nothing to spend them on here on this overgrown street, I throw them into the grass at the roadside, the ever-higher grass.

I won't find my diner. The houses are petering out, there are now just skeletons of houses, and some surviving old crosses in an old cemetery: they are proliferating, they are exponential crosses, with bifurcating side shoots like the antlers of old stags.

Then I reach the empty amphitheater, the benches of decaying wood, carpeted in last year's leaves: here the street ends. On the left, the referees' box high above, or maybe it's the concert bowl, is growing white, entirely coated in lime. Even the metal bullhorns way up top are bespattered in white. I run up the stairs, it's getting harder and harder to run, it's empty upstairs, lost pens lie scattered about.

I run down a slanting path to the other side, it's easy to run downwards. I'm running alone, without music, taking my time. At the foot of the white referees' box there are over a dozen wooden and cement blocks, carted here once, apparently, for some abandoned building project.

I place my hand on my heart: beneath my ribs I feel a silent stillness, the quiescence of a void. At that same instant, at the top of the referees' box, or the concert bowl, the lime-spattered bullhorn rings out with the amplified, rhythmic thud of a heart beating. Then I realize: that's my rhythm, the one that was urging me to go on, to run, and now it's over there, detached. I'm dead to such an extent that I don't even have the power of inertia that topples you to the ground, I am so lifeless that my standing posture is already conclusive.

The blocks of wood and cement begin to wobble, to rhythmically swing; they jostle each other with a rattling sound, they practically dance. The dead things are glad: I have descended to be one of them, from this moment on.

Outskirts on the Sands

There is amazing diversity in the sprouting of the local vegetation: in the pines and houses, the trees and buildings. The barren sands of the outlying districts, rising up to the surface here and there in the form of small deserts, favor the trees, which flourish and grow bigger than in the city. Yet at the same time, strangely enough, the homes shrivel in these same conditions, as if the ubiquitous pine roots had robbed them of their life-giving juices. And so the houses are stunted at their tar-blackened first floors, sapped of the strength to pile up into higher stories.

True, I've been warned that these are temporary districts, provisional neighborhoods, but I decided to live here nevertheless. My experience has taught me to believe in the unintended continuation of a provisional state, in the indestructability of things randomly thrown together. I made my decision, though my safety here is in no way guaranteed. Nonetheless . . . Fate had already taken so much away from me, almost all I owned on many occasions, that even if it were determined to do its worst with me, its loot would be miserably small, it would reap nothing at my expense. And thus, if there can be a certain satisfaction in poverty, I had found it.

I received an apartment on a public allotment. I found it empty, my precursor having already moved out. He must have scrupulously concealed his own poverty from himself: He left two things behind — curtains made of intricately snipped up crepe paper, a kind of imitation lace, as well as an empty demijohn painted to the neck with cherry-red oil paint. Had he really moved out? More likely he died, or better fortune, perhaps from abroad, had smiled upon him, otherwise he wouldn't have left me his imitation curtains and mock liqueur. This inheritance saved me from worrying about break-ins; I left the door unlocked; even if someone came in during my absence, he wouldn't take anything; my books wouldn't tempt him, unless it were a thief from a different district; everyone here is illiterate, and they wouldn't take books even for kindling, they can find enough dry twigs in the pine coppices.

And thus I live. I go on walks in search of resemblances

to things I once knew. If I find even their shadows, the day hasn't been a loss. That's how I link the present to the past; things whose roots somehow belong to the present day are indifferent to me, almost unnoticeable, beneath my attention. But that grocery-woman with frost-bitten cheeks, a cousin of the grand-grocery-woman from the Pink House, that acrid shadow luring earthworms and maple sprouts aboard last year's leaves; that whistle swirling the bewildered pigeons over the rooftops; those narrow-gauged railway tracks, between which even the stones turn to rust . . . These were important, worth remembering, simple recollection, the joy of recognition. This was enough, I would go back home, capable of nothing else, I would go through the unlocked door and see where my powerlessness was coming from: everything, whatever I did, would always be younger than me, accounted for, with no mystery of conception. The truth that could only be found in things predating myself was absent. I took comfort: Once the memory of arriving at the Sands had faded away, perhaps this area, washed clean by multiple rains, stripped of its colors by autumns and rejuvenated once again through springs, would somehow acclimatize to me, taking on the attributes of that everlastingness, as if it had taken me in years before and accepted me, and not I it. Would this happen? In any case, it would take a long time. And meanwhile, I didn't want to start anything from the beginning, I lived by striving for continuity, or its semblance.

Returning to the empty room from my walk, I would lie down on the bed between the stacks of books and dream up hypothetical continuations to stories which had abruptly concluded once and for all, as fate decided. And strangely enough, all of these speculations finished badly, contrary to my best intentions. I was only consoled by the awareness that any sort of catastrophe could be reversed by another speculation, that in this sphere everything was malleable. And at last sleep eased my mind, for I always had sober dreams, in which I wasn't a switchman for bygone events; they ran along their own tracks, and no flights of my imagination would make them jump the rails. I had sober dreams, but when I awoke from one of them, seemingly cured of the delusions of daylight, I saw a girl in the open doorway, in my doorway, and for the first moment I wasn't aware that she was irreversible, that she was real.

She didn't have the frost-bitten face of the green-grocer. Nor did she smell of dill. She was raven-haired and covered in beauty spots, and I wanted to know everything about her. I hoped that in finding out her origins and identity it wouldn't turn out that she had just then begun, so that I could at least in part count her as dear to me, encountered for the second time. Nothing in her many stories bolstered my hopes: she was new, and despite her complexion, her name was Anielka. She asked me to call her Angelica, and I complied with a certain unease, realizing that things like paper curtains and demijohns with pretend juice would be to her liking. For the first time I decided to lock the door, asking that she turn the key twice. As she moved naked to the door, I observed how her buttocks lifted lightly one after the other at every step, like the two melons the green-grocer had once placed on the trembling pans of a scale. And so! When she came back to where I stood, the black triangle where her thighs met was the moth that slept with folded wings, the Red Underwing, up to which I had crept in the garden of my childhood, holding my breath. Angelica turned out to be a collage of the mislaid scraps of my past, which I was then to rifle through day after day, night after night.

In time, Angelica was mastered bit by bit, our intimacy touched everything that had ever been. She prattled her monologues for hours in her delicate, slightly scratchy voice, not in fact requiring a listener or responses. I don't know what she was talking about, I didn't try to grasp the substance of her words, but that voice was a part of her, as indispensable as the murmur of the pine trees on the Sands. That was it: I was no longer searching for Angelica's foundations in my past, neither her prehistory nor her prototypes. I noticed that from the time she became the first-born amidst all my past and current things, she no longer came from them, but they began to come from her. That murmur, the murmur of the pines in the wind, was her whisper picked up by the landscape of our outskirts. Sometimes I would thank her, and when, in surprise, she asked what for, I would evasively respond that it was for arranging the books on the shelves or for closing the door, or something of the kind, as I understood the actual reasons for my gratitude were inexplicable.

Having assembled Angelica from those elements that I myself had scraped together, I had no idea there was more to her, that Angelica could have within her something unto herself and independent of me. We were sitting in front of the window, it was a yellow autumn, and the window was no more covered by the paper curtains; in its place, Angelica had hung her blue shirt, specially cut up from top to bottom, imitating a patch of clear blue sky; the real sky on that day was dirty-gray.

"What have you been doing these past years?" I asked.

"Whoring myself."

"What do you mean?!"

"It was nothing special, just for pleasure."

From then on, whenever I went out I locked her in the room, and for the first time in my life I started to learn faith in the future, I, a fanatical advocate of the pre-existing world. The present day, which had always been for me merely the crowning achievement of the past, from that moment became no more than the germ of what lay in store for us, released from its own prehistory. I poured water into the red demijohn and put some flowers in it; for pleasure, for her pleasure. One day I brought home a bouquet: small violet asters.

I knocked on the door, and again, and once more, then many times. She wouldn't open up, and we had only one key between us, which I had left her that day. She wouldn't open up. "Angelica!" I cried, "Angelica! It's me!" From next door an unfamiliar neighbor peeked out, with an old face all the more wrinkled from sympathy; it disappeared, and then came back to offer me a chair, as if to kindly sentence me to long, fruitless knocking in a seated position. I shoved away the chair and again cried, "Angelica! Open up, I can hear you whispering, I know you're not alone, I bet your uncle dropped by, why don't you want to introduce me to your uncle, open up, my asters are wilting, the violet kind you like, Angelica, don't fool around, because I'll never leave you the key again, why are you teasing me, you know, they're going to put in new housing blocks here, we'll get an apartment with a bathroom, our hut is scheduled to be demolished, have you gone nuts, Anielka?"

Then I crawled in through an open courtyard window. And that, I suppose, would be it. No one was whispering in the room, it was only the pines murmuring on the Sands. At first I thought she was playing a dumb joke, that she was hiding somewhere; I looked under the bed and under the blankets: nothing. On the sheets there was the only trace of her: a black, spiraling hair. Even the curtains made of her blue shirt weren't there, neither on the window nor anywhere else. Yes. That meant it was time to move on, to somewhere entirely different, after all, I'd been warned that this was only temporary, I'd been shown the blueprints for the new district. And there, in that completely different place, would I have enough strength to betray myself, to search no more for the resemblances to the only things that were true, because I had always known them? Could you wonder at someone who, watching everything fall to pieces time and again, bundles those scraps into a single whole, in order to finally trust in something, albeit something that once was . . . But was it once for certain?

Perhaps you can't demand sobriety from everyone. That would be cruel. When I left with a suitcase filled with odds and ends (Anielka hadn't taken a thing!) and I trudged through the sand towards town, I realized that my home-spun theories on the truth of pre-existing events didn't make a bit of sense, that I was and always had been an advocate of things lost. It was hard to go, it might have been easier if in escaping Anielka had taken everything with her, not just because my suitcase would have been lighter, but you know, in general.

My Forest

My forest is fenced in; a forest should not be fenced in. I have the key to my forest. Otherwise you can only get to it from above, and so my forest is only open to birds, squirrels and the rain. It is mainly filled with pines, acacias and coalmice. In the midst of it all stands a house which is uninhabitable. It has no floor or furnishings; it would be empty, were it not full of intentions. Under the pines stands an unhitched Gypsy caravan, carved in dragons and colors. It has gone down all of its roads and its presence here, its woodland inertia, has allowed me to believe that while in my forest I am everywhere. In the summer nights I sleep in the caravan, and my dreams totter and creak like the ungreased axles of the wheels, dreams of different shapes and colors.

I was unaware that, cut off from the forest-at-large, my forest would eventually grow stunted, that in continually maintaining the semblance of a forest it would become at best a copse, tamed by force. For the moment, there was nothing foretelling that process. I grew up in the city, but for years I have returned now and again to the legacy of my forefathers: my grandfather, and his father and grandfather, had been rangers. I saw this as the forest lineage from which I was descended, and I wanted to live up to it.

One had to turn from geometry to irrationality: after all, this is the essence of a forest. This shift came to me easily: I went to the vast forest, known locally as the state forest, and surrendering myself to it, I started to get lost, as is my habit. I walked barefoot through the strewn pine needles and cones, a mosaic of sharp edges. When I sat down on a stump, staring at my heels that were aromatic and crimson from squashed wild strawberries, I realized that I was in an uncharted location on earth. And that is also the essence of a forest, a true forest. Birds were only rarely visible, they flew down from high above, scarcely audible. I had learned from Father, who was fostered by the forest, to identify some by their diverse and melodious calls. How far I had come from the concrete blocks of civilization! My untrodden path led nowhere, it only knew its way between the pines. All the nearby village names, names of the settlements at the edge of the forest — Zuzela, Leśne, Zawisty — forfeited their referents here, became little more than birdsongs.

That's how I served my green apprenticeship, the training for full authority over my forest, fenced in and closed off. With time I started to notice mushrooms with tawny, edible flesh, and white dimples where snails had nibbled. Then I could come back home. I was ready. The forest guided me out of its heart, where the compass held no sway.

My forest awaited me, fenced off from all four sides. When I entered, I wasn't surrounded by pine trunks, as happens in a forest, the trees were each singular and countable. Someone rattled the gate. It was the deaf old man, the berry-picker, whom the gamekeeper had once mistaken for a badger.

"You have very nice trees," he complimented me. "Like in a forest. They've seen a few years."

Trees! I have trees, and they've seen a few years, years nourished by time, much as the water flowing through streams nourishes stones. They might have seen as many as sixty years in the wild. The old man had a tin quart-bucket in his basket filled with dark blueberries and some wild strawberries. I bought a liter of blueberries: I love *pierogi** with blueberries.

From that moment on, turning against its own nature, my forest started to lose its inborn shade, it fell silent;

though the sap effusions still smelled of pine. It might have started earlier, I must have overlooked the first signs, but now it had intensified and swollen. I was gripped by a woodcutter's phobia: the sudden panic that, at any moment, the trunks of my pines would come toppling down on me. Nothing of the sort. Nothing had changed, the perpendiculars were intact, it was only that the birds weren't singing. The wind shook the treetops. I was no woodcutter, let them stand, there's no sense in felling captive trees.

When on the following day I peeked out from my wagon, the moss and the pine needles were carpeted with fowl. It seems they had fallen from the trees with the onset of the night, like worm-eaten apples, diminutive and exaggeratedly colorful. They were mainly yellowish-gold orioles, spotted thrushes and robins, as bright as agaric. I collected them all up and buried them beneath some junipers.

Aunt Fruzia

Aunt Fruzia rose from the dead in order to serve dinner. She gathered herself up from a dozen or so objects that had been stuffed into corners and drawers, completed herself with a final component pulled from the wardrobe, and began to function. She had become a fully intentional composition, independent of fashion, and thus, notwithstanding her on-and-off existence, she was the sole guarantor of the stability of our life and the regulator of the hours which had wandered astray from the clock.

Aunt Fruzia's Bible, her cookbook, were it to be looked at with a discerning eye, contained complete guidelines for behavior, formed a universal selection of recipes for living.

And thus the verse which often appeared on its pages: "And stew covered on a low flame," was perhaps Aunt Fruzia's main motto, a motto which in practice ensured propriety in life and the kitchen.

We got used to those auntish activities, so all-encompassing as to be imperceptible. Only on a day like today, at a birthday party, could Auntie demonstrate (albeit invisibly, like a deity) her inexhaustible omnipotence. Every culinary act of creation was saturated with her individuality, to such an extent that in savoring her herring salad or leavened cakes with rose-petal frosting we committed cannibalism, we became man-eating gourmands. Small wonder that later, under the pretence of a migraine, Aunt Fruzia, or to be precise, her indestructible remainder, shut herself up in her dark room to slowly and painstakingly consolidate, replenish her painful losses, however and with whatever means. Then she would appear in the dining room when all the guests had left and gone home. Wilted, long deprived of her youthful charms, she had her own well-founded reasons for not coming under the scrutiny of her company until they were well fed.

And then at the end of the visit she accepted the tributes and praises with flushed cheeks, while gathering up the dirty plates and cutlery, to announce the end of the dining ceremony with a clatter. Only her closest relatives had not moved from their seats: Uncle Tymek and his wife Polcia, dressed according to the latest Australian fashions, in creations sent from time to time by a cousin in Sydney, as well as myself and the host. And then came the time when Aunt Fruzia, freed from her gastronomical functions, somewhat regenerated and still devoted to her principles, turned to us to make her eager preparations.

We knew that none of us would escape, neither Tymek with his silence nor Polcia with her false admiration, mumbling, "Well I never! I never!" Aunt Fruzia now commenced with the disembowelments. It was difficult to outwardly oppose her. So much of her substance, contained in culinary masterstrokes, had vanished into our depths that her actions seemed like a legal attempt at revindication. Maybe she didn't even want to get anything back, but required only reciprocity, or longed to restore the strength that had been consumed? I don't know. Only one thing was indisputably clear: she was beginning her disembowelments. She performed them discreetly, to one side, having her tête-à-tête with each of us in turn. She rummaged about in our insides with the routine manner of a cook, deftly avoiding the spleens of our objections and defenses, extracting these untouched with all the rest, so as not to spoil the taste of the dish she had an appetite for . . . the taste of our closest confidences.

Is this what she had been feeding us for, flattering our palates only to feed on us in turn, down to the soft lining of our essences, unto the shameful mucous membrane of our subconsciousnesses? After these initial procedures, she got to the heart of the matter; Uncle Tymek was first up to be stewed covered over a low flame. He sat hunched over, already hollow from having had all his contents torn out, as Aunt Fruzia proceeded with her plan. She spent very little time on him, not because he was holding himself back, but because he evidently was none too filling. She left him shipwrecked in the corner, and next started on his wife, Polcia, leaving me for last.

She was my mother's sister, and thus there ought to have been in her a shade of the distaff side, of kindness and understanding. And yet I could not bear her parasitical ways, her extractiveness. I made a secret decision. I had heard of a primitive but effective folk method of weaning a child from the mother's breast, a method which involved sprinkling pepper on the nipple. I resolved to use an analogous trick, believing that I would give my aunt a lasting distaste for dining on me, or, at the very least, a chronic case of indigestion. In spite of everything, I was better off than a plucked hen: I could simulate my contents, dream up whole reams of imaginary biography . . . and let Auntie prey on them.

This is what I did that very evening. Auntie's obvious gluttony, her evident rapacity inspired me to all the more extravagant multiplications of fictions, to their unbridled autogeny. As an example, allow me to repeat the last fragment of the birthday confession. I said:

"These words get caught in my throat, but I want to be

sincere with you. My conscience aches for having said nothing of this earlier, for having kept it bottled up within me till today. The fault is mine; I believe you will forgive me when I've confessed everything. I was eighteen years old and, you recall, you and Mother wanted to have me admitted to the priest in Biecz, to the parish monastery. Never and nowhere since have I encountered such a concentration of solemnity. The church and monastery were almost Gothic, despite the pure Baroque of the walls, thanks to the slender trees of the surrounding park, mainly thujas and Italian poplars. There was an extraordinary heat wave that year, and even the river couldn't cool you off any more. In days like those, the most refreshing place on earth was the church, inside the church. I would soak in the stream of coolness with its smell of stock gillyflowers, which was an act of God's mercy accessible to the senses. It was empty in the gloomy interior, and only a blundering bumblebee battering itself against the stained glass filled the naves with its pious drone, in place of the mute organs. One day, by the side altar (it was around noon) I saw a nun, or more exactly, her back cloaked in a habit and her pair of pink heels peeking out of their sandals. She knelt, absorbed in prayer. I had already stared more than once at all the pictures, sculptures, the Stations of the Cross, everything that was and was not worth looking at in that church. With that same expectation I moved nearer, so as to somehow link this nun to the surrounding collection of sacral art.

"She lifted her head and then immediately let it fall. I remember only that her eyes had one black brow ranging from temple to temple; and that she was very beautiful. A moment later she crossed herself, and the church was filled with the slapping sound of quickly departing sandals. I followed her almost mechanically, over the church doorstep, through a passage of blinding sunlight and a small trellis that was green and shady. She went into a stairwell, ran down a long corridor, and vanished. I chased after her and found myself before the open door to an empty refectory; the long corridor stretched on further, with many identical black doors on either side. They were all shut. I was afraid to just knock on the first one, as I might have been asked to leave. So I tiptoed back and forth, back and forth, vainly searching for some sign to set apart my nun's door from the rest."

Uncle Tymek stood and started to say his goodbyes, Polcia was fixing herself up with some Australian lipstick before setting off. I paused in my confession of events that had never happened. Aunt Fruzia said goodbye more curtly than usual and a moment later turned back to me. I said:

"I gave up my search and just tried to imagine her . . . to imagine her entirely, and please understand me literally. Yet it is exceedingly difficult, essentially impossible to reconstruct the whole solely based on two known fragments like a pair of pink heels and a connected black eyebrow emphasizing the forehead. And then all of a sudden, at the opposite end of the corridor, a door half opened and I saw the flash of a pale hand and a black eyebrow. I ran over: the door had already shut, but on the stone floor lay a piece of paper folded in four. It was for me, I hadn't the slightest doubt, though the nun had addressed it 'To the Unknown Pilgrim.' She invited me to rendezvous at the door to her cell at 9:00 in the evening, assuring me that she only hoped to converse in the spirit of love for one's neighbor. I was punctual and she was punctual. Please take my word that I would prefer to forget all this, or at any case conceal it as the most shameful secret weighing upon my soul. I won't hide anything from you. But please forgive me in advance if I do not pay scrupulous attention to detail in relating the train of events. They are buried in the depths of my memories, in a place that is still breathless, despite the years gone by, memories that to this day are more in control of me than I am of them.

"I entered and bowed, and greeted her without taking her hand. The matter with which she had come to me was very simple: Sister Eleonora (or thus she introduced herself to me) asked me to assist her in, as she put it, an 'innocent sin.' She wanted me to deliver her sister, a secular woman living in Raciąż, a letter from her. The nuns from this cloister were not allowed to carry on a correspondence with the world left behind. She only wanted me to buy an envelope, address it, put the letter inside, affix the stamps and send it. 'The least I could do,' I said, 'the least I could do.' Somehow it sounded as though I wanted to say that I was ready for more serious, more imperative services or favors. Sister Eleonora lowered her gaze as though embarrassed, and we both fell silent. She didn't seem to be showing me to the door, but our subject of conversation had run dry.

"I stood leaning against the wall, at the head of an iron bed covered with a gray blanket, and I searched for the words that would allow me to continue our discussion. Through the window, of which only the top pane was uncovered, the green shadow of a branch swayed rhythmically. The pendulum of the wall clock swung at the same slow tempo. Sister Eleonora stared at that shadow and that clock, and gradually she herself was filled with the measured rhythm: she started, perhaps unaware, to sway from side to side, from side to side, as if jolted by that time, which was systematically and passionlessly trampling her, the same time that dwells in the gears of mechanical toys.

"I won't excuse myself for what came next. Maybe it was just a question of that rhythm, embracing one thing after another in its power, the rhythm in the face of which I could not stay indifferent, which I had to join. Sister Eleonora's rhythm was none of her doing, nor did mine come from me. Both were clearly only resonances, ripples of the flow of time, of the very same time. Only her heels were pink, as well as her mouth and ears, her ripening ears which grew brighter and brighter. Her legs kicked in the air, as if they wanted to push away its all-revealing transparency, or perhaps they were defending themselves from a Satan who remained invisible to me, whose panting breath filled the whole cell. Her hands, which lay still in mine, were defenseless against his diabolical ploys. Instead of her hands, her imploring breasts rose up towards heaven, stiffening upwards, and if they hadn't come up against my body they would certainly have grown into a second pair of hands cursing her fate. Perhaps her navel was most beautiful of all, but her long crucifix hanging from a hempen string obscured it every other minute. And when she suddenly clung to me, she began to scream. No, that was no scream, it was a soaring and rapturous song, filled with branching cadences of words. She sang in Latin!"

Thus more or less ran one of several of my confessions to Aunt Fruzia. She sat disarmed, her eyes shifting back and forth. Then she picked herself up and, overlooking one plate that had yet to be cleaned, left to her room. I thought my story had taken its effect, that I was free from her endless gluttony. And indeed, I was free once and for all. Could I have imagined that the fodder I had served my aunt would be so toxic that it would prove fatal?

She was found the following day clutching her cookbook to her motionless heart. In fact, she wasn't such a bad woman. I say this not because I offended her so terribly. The fact is that following her demise, this final one, from which she didn't manage to resurrect herself even in bits and pieces, our life lost its stability, the cake with rose-petal frosting vanished once and for all, and we were left to the mercies and miseries of impassive clocks.

An Alliance

"Take this watermelon!" she cried, struggling to lift her arms, her fingertips all turned white from the strain of the imaginary weight. "Take it, take it!"

This was unbearable; we had always been so close, and now we both found ourselves in different places, in entirely different places. This is why she cried out so loud, in fear of her voice not reaching me from such a great distance. Even though I was sitting right next to her, full of a restless conscience, prepared to hear even a whisper. She was on her own, without me, between the tropics of her own fever.

It was twilight. At the head of the bed burned a lamp

with a tea shade, inside it a fly was battering itself in a cramped flight punctuated with silences, its vast shadow fluttering around the wardrobe and the walls. I couldn't give Maria any relief. An impenetrable thicket of trembling had grown between us, through which I had no passage. Only Maria's hurried breathing hacked through it, vainly searching for a place she could take refuge.

She had stopped calling out to me, she was silent. She grappled alone with that strange weight, the heavier for all my betrayal. Locks of her hair, scattered over the pillow, convulsively twisted and straightened themselves out. What must have been going on inside her! I bustled about, squeezing a lemon, pouring water into a glass, pouring it into a second glass, I had to do something, action replaced by movement, any movement would do. This watchfulness alone, silent like quicksilver in a thermometer, was not enough. I mechanically poured liquid from one glass to another: it got colder and colder; finally it started to chill my hand. It was a peculiar hourglass measuring out the hours; but I had already stopped counting them, I had lost track. The night hung in Maria's empty, raised hands, but was thrown off balance by the glow from the lamp. The knotholes in the wardrobe's right-hand door, always blind and closed, unfurled themselves, I myself don't know when, and stared, weeping sap. I suddenly saw that both my glasses had run dry, that I was pouring nothing but thin air, that measurable time was now exhausted to the last drop.

The shadow of what might have been a rook flapped silently from wall to wall: it was looking for a nest! I was not going to be that nest, not for anything in the world!

I threw a glance at Maria, our gazes crossed and, for the first time, we came to an understanding: she wasn't going to be a nest either, not for anything in the world. Our shared dread was our support, a guide for the imminent journey through the underbrush of the fever, the chaparral of shivers. The nightlamp less blinded us than burned our eyes. I didn't understand. What was she waiting for? What darkness did she want to endure? "Maria," I whispered, and Maria heard that whisper. She answered me with a look that pleaded for help.

In her sagging arms hung a huge watermelon. I grabbed it with both hands just seconds before it fell. Maria's arms immediately dropped to her sides. We'll split it. I got a knife and cut the fruit in half. No longer a torment, it relieved our thirst. The pulp was sky-blue, and the seeds the color of saffron. I bit into my half. Such bitterness! Too bitter for her.

Maria's arms lay peacefully on the quilt. Exhausted from her many hours of lifting, she slept.

Gorissia

Though as yet I had no idea how many eras the Gorysz region* had seen, or that the town had had its name for untold centuries, noted down in the ancient Roman chronicles as Gorissia, I had already noticed the intriguing erosion of the landscape. All the edges are frayed at the corners, the colors have worn away like old frescos. Over the Gorysz market square stretches the main path of bird migration, and during all four seasons of the year feathery processions cut a wide swath of white in the sky.

The centuries have taken their toll: the essence of the town has been diluted in the solution of eternally trickling time; stripped of regenerative strength, it is becoming ever more barren. This has endowed the landscape with an impotent gentleness, I would even say a somnolent giddiness. The town archives have long disappeared, the stones have been struck dumb, but Gorysz carries on, without memory or origins. Since the discovery of natural gas fifteen or so kilometers away the youth have cleared out, returning only once a week to drink up their earnings in the town's tavern, Under the Red Bottle. The restaurant was Gorysz's sole concession to the industrialization of the district. In the former town hall, on the Gothic ogive over the main entrance, a neon sign shaped like a bottle glows red after dusk.

This was perhaps the only gesture of reconciliation. The young people drank their due and then took flight in a factory bus with a hurried stampede, fearing the duplicitous local time, which though seeming to doze in stagnation was as all-devouring as a swamp. The locals seldom leave their homes; they mostly sit by their closed windows on either side of the narrow streets, noses pressed to the panes, observing each other's expectations. This strained two-way vigilance, multiplying itself infinitely like the thousandfold depths of two mirrors set opposite one another, is no longer a waiting for something; it has instead become a relentless process of aging.

Their past is a blank. They depart into it, one after another, as though going into the night. The windows become deserted. In this forsaken nothingness, the sole road signs are the gravestones. Every funeral is an act of populating this desert of time passed. The soil is quite adept at receiving, but lifts nothing back onto the surface; wasting away on the outside, it keeps all its potencies in its depths. Only we, the archaeologists, know of this, and it was this that convinced me to make this journey, to start this search. Only we strangers could suspect that at the roots of this motionless landscape proliferated the underground Gorysz, that the rupturing urns were ripening like truffles.

In this town, or more accurately, in this village, for Gorysz had lost its town status, penetrated and stripped bare by the passing of time, I decided that whatever the cost I would bring something to the light of day, something that had escaped intact from the ubiquitous, disillusioned tedium, something which the stumbling plod of generations of pedestrians had not managed to stamp out. In digging I expected to find urns, and so the appearance of a skeleton from beneath the layers of sand was a surprise. It lay on its side, with knees folded under its chin, and in its jaws sat thirty-two teeth untouched by decay. There could be no doubt that I had uncovered a Neolithic grave of the Brzesko-Kujawska culture.* I was carefully cleaning bone after bone with a brush when a legless old man in a wheelchair appeared at the edge of the excavation site. He stared at the skeleton for a long moment through his thick eyeglasses. "My God!" he sighed. "My God, so young!" Then he crossed himself, and taking up a handful of sand, threw it into the excavation pit and went off.

I already knew Gorysz and its inhabitants fairly well, I knew of their carelessness in living and scrupulousness in dying. And so I wasn't surprised at the old man's gesture. His life was already no more than a semblance, that handful of sand was not so much a payment of final respects as a sign of solidarity with the dead. I grasped this at once, which is why I didn't yell at the old man, though his sand had scattered over the skull I had just cleaned. It could be that I'm more of an archaeologist than an authority on people: the muteness of that skeleton said more than the silence of the Goryszians. I understood its odd position, the correct placement of the mortal remains in accordance with ancient custom, I fit it neatly into its appropriate category. Enough for today. Using crates and boards I safeguarded the find from the cats that are forever multiplying in Gorysz, filling the drowsy streets with their sweetish stench.

In Under the Red Bottle I ordered a pork chop and some mineral water to wash my hands with. There was no water from the rusted faucet, and my hands were black from the soil. I drew a rough map of Gorysz on a napkin, then the excavation site, and finally the grave itself. These were unhandsome drawings, careless, drawn for a letter to my sister, which I wanted to send as soon as possible, to share the joy of my success. Behind the window a reddish darkness had already fallen: the neon bottle had risen in the Gothic ogive that seemed specially made for it. My pork chop still hadn't arrived, despite the fact that I was alone in the dining room and there were at least two waitresses. Both the first and then the second approached me with the same explanation: it's frying.

I wrote to my sister: "You know I've had more important finds . . . the ceremonial circle near Sieradz,* or the burial ground of face urns . . . and yet perhaps this Gorysz skeleton pleases me the most. The boredom here, stifling and heavy, stretching open the mouths of the natives into toothless yawns, has raised the importance of my find through its contrast; you know, it's as if the deep Neolithic layer has brought life to the mortuary of the surface. This is no less important to me than its strictly scientific significance." I can't say how long my hunger battled the exhaustion that eventually overcame it. Apart from myself, the place was empty. I gave one last shot at the pork chop, or at least at paying for the mineral water: I started insistently tapping the bottle with a coin.

My signal sounded in the empty restaurant like the bell of a choirboy, a glass treble. But after a moment it was filled out with a music of deep resonance, a brass gong, as if the silence, recklessly broken, tapped by my two-złoty piece, was shattering into an expanding rumble of self-annihilation. I tore myself from the table, but the ringing played on. I ran to the counter, but there was nobody around, only a cat sleeping in the glass display case. I ran out. The whole darkness swung with the music of the bells and the flickering of the candles in the street. A funeral procession was approaching.

I join the mourning entourage; I walk faster than the other mourners, passing them by, drawing nearer to the two-wheeled hearse. Right behind it is the legless old man in his wheelchair, the two waitresses from Under the Red Bottle are pushing him and lighting the way with candles. The rest of them I have never seen before; or at least there was no way to tell them apart, with their staring eyes and furrows in their cheeks deep as scars. A tin plaque wobbles on the coffin, now leaning into the light, now into the darkness. I read: Anon. Citizen of the City of Gorysz.

Incredible how all-encompassing Goryszian anonymity is! After a nameless life deprived of any distinguishing features, after everything, they don't let it be known what their names were. Perhaps so that the memory of them, too, would be nameless? Maybe then they can more easily bear the final departure, after which those remaining are much like those absent? Like sparrows, which are in fact one sparrow, multiplied into an innumerable swarm of identical copies . . . The tin had already been stuck into a hillock of sand which rose above the fresh grave. People started to disperse in groups, snuffing out their candles. I had with me a flashlight, a source of light that I reckoned was too secular for this occasion. I remained a bit longer at the cemetery, and only after everyone else had left, having waited a moment, I started walking back down the road to the tavern, where I had a room on the first floor. Soon I could turn off my flashlight: the glow of the red bottle was enough. As I walked I had a strange sensation: I thought to myself that I didn't regret the additional trip to the cemetery, that it had been one of very few opportunities to make contact with the residents of Gorysz, and that soon perhaps nobody would have such a chance, in this near-deserted backwater town, slowly stagnating to archaeology. Passing the excavation site I glanced into my hole. The sandy bottom of the Neolithic grave was entirely bare.

Intermission

The silence wasn't independent and distinct, it was an abyss at the foot of the last explosion, as steep as a mountain touching the sky. We were falling in that bottomless abyss, silently like in a dream, uncertain if the bombardment had already finished, or if the next explosion would lift us again a moment later. None of the many initial moments could vouch for the one to follow, but at last we trusted the silence. The pink light of the fire that had passed us peeked in through the windows, like the dawn foretelling a sunny day. Here we are, we thought, and for the first time we felt honored to be deemed fit for *being*.

Teresa got up and nodded at me suggestively from the

threshold: Let's go. I shrugged my shoulders; now, when I'm all at loose ends, when I couldn't even swallow a sip of coffee? It's not that Teresa was fearless, she simply loved to violate a silence, to come out of a bombardment intact, more intact, fuller than usual. Lance Corporal Wyga went instead of me, and it wasn't long before I heard Teresa's gasping moans from behind the wall, sounding much like the whimper of the wounded.

I knew it was only an intermission, that nothing had finished and that everyone knew it, though they wanted to somehow take root in it. I could not. For me a silence was a hatchery of terror, because every explosion was conceived in one. Maybe I would have started speaking of the past if I had had someone to listen, but Solon and Benek had already started to play twenty-one, and Wyga had gone off with Teresa. This much I could do: revive the past, and pass it on to someone else, thus reconfirming my faith that the topography of the future would be similar, in a word, that a future would exist at all, that this would be a certainty. But for this I needed listeners with at least silent credulity; it was too difficult for me to believe myself alone, because I knew my own hope-spinning strategies all too well.

After three days and nights of unrelenting action, we were sent here for a rest. We received permission to sleep, an affirmative for a short desertion of consciousness. But there was no question of sleeping, so I decided to go out and sober up in the chill of the night. A month and a half had passed since the start of the uprising, but that September night had no chill to it, it was feverish, heated by two burning streets: the one on the left and its cross street, and maybe ones further on as well. The names of those streets were unfamiliar to me; in the past I had only seldom visited this district, and later on . . . Our roads didn't fall in line with the directions of the city streets, they ran through breaches in walls, through cellars and connecting trenches. I wouldn't be able to even approximately locate those passages on a city map.

I didn't know where I was going, I had only made a decision not to leave the zone marked out by the pink glow pulsating from the fires. There was no need to grope about here, while further on there was only the impenetrable darkness. After the onslaught of artillery fire and bombs, the silence had been so overwhelming that one would have been inclined to chalk it up to one's own deafness were it not for the distant bursts of machine gun fire, which now had an almost idyllic sound, like the monotonous chirping of grasshoppers.

I had come out to breathe the fresh air and found I couldn't breathe. Though the breeze was carrying the smoke in the opposite direction, the air was stifling and it was getting more stifling by the minute, as if in an ever more perfect vacuum. As long as there was time left I intended to scrape together the silence, lay it out to dry like good soporific herbs, which might dispel the rumble or at least make it gentler. But I couldn't, I wouldn't stock up any reserves. We'd been had. To think that I didn't see through the swindle from the start . . . I, an authority on silence, a researcher into its consistency and varieties. No, nobody had steered me wrong. I had let myself be taken in. I found neither a voluptuous and submissive silence here, the maiden of my idleness, nor a silence heaping like a snow-drift, keeping intruders at bay from my peaceful dreams. I wouldn't find it, because this was no time, here and now, for this most skittish of the natural elements. What surrounded me was not silence, but the lack of a rumble, a hollow place after a sound and after the silence, a vast and deep rupture with no shores and no bottom.

Again I recalled an image that for a week I had been trying to ward off with all my might: Wacek lying in the grass. Sunbathing, his shirt unbuttoned. And suddenly there was an enormous dragonfly with great big eyes, all emerald and sapphire. It sits on his forehead, throwing a veiny and transparent shadow on his cheek: it is hunting for the flies that have been spiralling about here in growing numbers. So far I suspected nothing, while they knew everything already, buzzing about to mimic the whizz of bullets, one of which Wacek failed to hear. And now the hollowness that came after the sound grew overwhelming, as if it wanted to push me down onto that grass, supine, fill me up with itself, like I was fly-bait . . .

At the intersection of two side streets a cool breeze

reached me. I turned to where it seemed to be emanating from, as if I could cross from the scorching heat to the realm of shade. Some stairs led me down to the basement of a burning apartment building, in which the residents from all the floors were taking shelter by the light of a few candles. It was no ordinary shelter, but a potential cemetery, a catacombs, the moment before it was walled up and the grave lights extinguished. I found myself on the threshold; the one audience to that dress rehearsal for mass necrosis. Seizing advantage of the intermission, there had begun intensive training for dying, trying on motionlessness for size, a formulating of final silences.

They lay crowded on plank beds and straw mattresses, staring at the low ceiling made of charred brick, waiting for the closing of their eyelids in mute acceptance of everything that was happening. I looked around and, in a sudden flash, recognized Professor Deresz, a state junior high-school inspector. Had it not been for his beard, long and perhaps red, I would have recognized him straight away.

"Professor," I whispered, "What are you doing here?"

In response he swiveled his eyes towards an empty mattress.

"No Professor!" I protested, "It can't be!"

"We're all mortal," said Deresz. "And in circumstances such as these . . . especially mortal."

"Please leave, Professor," I whispered. "The building is

burning, the fire has already spread down to the second floor."

"Shhh!" came a hissing from the neighboring plank beds, which were dark, unilluminated by the candlelight. "Good night."

Professor Deresz propped himself up on an elbow, wanting to snuff out his candle. He came right up to it with his mouth and blew, he blew with all of his lungs . . . but the flame didn't even tremble, it stood lifeless, stiff as a dart. Poor Professor. It was clear he didn't realize how much he had waned, to what extent he had stopped mattering. Both he and all the others had depleted themselves so entirely that the rest was just hollow formality, an epilogue without greater significance.

"Don't get upset, Professor," I said, "I insulted you by accusing you of inertia. Now I think I see how much it cost you to prepare for nonexistence, to nurture it from within yourself. I'm sorry, now I see that you didn't want to trust in chance, to be taken by surprise. It is you who are the rebel. And I? I will take risks to live, I will even take risks, Professor."

Deresz half opened his lips and moved them without making a sound. This was no doubt his response. His face hastily went through all the successive phases of a silent argument; the severely etched marks of his wrinkles and furrows arranged themselves now in constellations of high seriousness, now irony, now in an alphabet of ignorance full of question marks. And they fluttered away like great mosquitos to a flame, stripping Deresz's face of its last scraps of meaning.

I grabbed the candle and held it over my head. From all the now-illuminated plank beds reflected the shine of faces that had been entirely abandoned, shorn of even their features; they were eyeless lumps of blind wax.

The candle trembled; stearin flowed down the back of my hand and onto my wrist. If I hadn't seen it happen, I wouldn't have known at all — there was no burning sensation. Was death so contagious? I dropped the candle and I don't know myself how I got out of there — faster, faster! — to the door, and then up the stairs.

Good God! Where had I been? My gun had remained at our quarters, Solon was keeping an eye on it. I went towards the quarters, or to where I thought they were: every direction, painted in that same glow, looked identical. I didn't so much walk as drag myself forward, feeling the radiance, the parching redness in the eyes, on the tongue, all over me, like clotted blood.

I was almost there when it started. It was less an explosion than a relentless thunder that shattered the night into pieces, splintered further by the clatter of machine guns. It happened at just the moment when I thought the vacuum would choke me. I breathed quickly and greedily, I breathed with fear as pure as ozone, completely transformed into the running, the crawling, the licking of earth from my lips that had gone salty from sweat. Finally: Solon and my gun, which had started to bark in the night. I was afraid of every moment, every fraction of a second. I was saved.

They Don't Ring at the Bernardines'

The downpour caught me in the dead center of 20th of February Square. Not having an umbrella, I took a short cut straight to the Bernardines'. In the slanting streams of rain the church bent all the perpendiculars of its façade, wet pigeons slumped in all its rafters. Soaked to the skin, I made it to the church gates: they were shut. I managed to get in by a side entrance through the sacristy, and right by the door I was greeted by a large inscription: NO SMOKING. I removed my hat. A thick tobacco smell quite unlike any church incense I knew wafted towards me.

It was nearly empty. Only the handful of pews in the main nave held some praying parishioners. There were neither statues, nor crucifixes, nor altars. Between the columns, in portals stripped of their Baroque, shelves loaded down with tobacco leaves hieratically rose upwards. Who were they praying to? I stood inside, the rainwater trickling off me, pooling into a puddle on a flagstone that had grown concave from centuries of footfalls. The music of the rain filled the church with an evangelical whisper.

This lasted a few moments. Soon everybody got up and went towards the exit. I stepped aside to let them by, elderly people who came right at me like they were blind. I stuck out an arm to keep a hobbling old man from colliding with me, but he kept going. He went through me without so much as a jostle, as if I were no more than space; he swept through me, as would a wave of heat or a chill, he spanned my width with his tiny steps and hobbled on, his shoes tracking my rainwater further along the flagstones. I felt like a corridor, a double exit, a path of no resistance to the outside world. The old man vanished behind a wall. He must have developed the most radical consequences of blindness: The whole world he had turned a blind eye to had lost its real consistency, had stopped existing even in theory, so as to open up in all directions, to annihilate all obstacles on the road leading from darkness to darkness.

I backed up against the wall and leaned on it with my whole body, for the first time drawing satisfaction from its impenetrable solidity, defining my limits and autonomy, strengthening my shaken faith.

All the saints had left here long ago, no doubt, on some remote day of eviction. But they don't see this, they haven't come to terms with this, just as they don't recognize my presence, my very existence. Right next to me lay the stone leg of a sarcophagus and part of a tablet with golden letters.

I tried to decipher it, to reconstruct the whole of the Latin inscription. And suddenly I was frightened by my own intentions. No, I wouldn't complete the leg or the golden letters. They could have drawn me in, resurrected, to the brotherhood of the dark-sighted parishioners, for whom only the past is visible. Below the cracked wall painting depicting the Assumption of the Holy Virgin, from inside a confessional full of carved-wood ornaments, someone nodded at me. It was a priest disfigured by smallpox scars that had changed his face into a shapeless lump, so that the Creator could begin anew on His sculpture of human physiognomy. I thought that he wanted me to confess, that he was inviting me to kneel. I didn't care to; but he cried to me:

"Come in!"

I didn't understand what he wanted, but he pulled me by the sleeve and sat me in the confessional, then he pushed an elevator button and we started going up, past the ascending Mother of God with a scrape of paint and plaster, only to surpass her and rise higher.

We got out into the bell tower. The rain here was more present, more sonorous.

"Landetur Jesus Christus," I said.

"In saecula saeculorum," came the choral response. "These are the words of today's Holy Gospel: a wide barometrical depression is shifting from over the Belarus region, carrying with it a profuse rainfall, disappearing or decreasing to a drizzle in the west. Strong northeastern winds. Amen."

"Here, at the highest point of the temple, we know best," said the pockmarked priest, leading me to the window.

At the peak of the main tower nearby, the spinning cross indicated the direction of the wind with its arms, creaking loudly in the strong gusts. In the twilight some dim figures swarmed about; I could not tell if they were Baroque statues, or priests, or perhaps clerks from tobacco factory storehouses.

"And when does the good priest expect it to clear up?" I asked.

"Oh, none too soon, none too soon," he said, folding his hands. "Only after the deluge, when down there, on the earth, the tobacco gets wet."

There on the earth! It was true, I was in the highest reaches of the church, but it was also the basement of the heavens, a living quarters for God's servants. Here the rains could only pass us by. But what about them?

"And the parishioners, Father? They're praying down there! We'd better ring the bells to warn them!"

"Not so fast, my son, not so fast," he said warmly. "You're taking them too seriously, too literally. That would have been proper thirty years ago, or let's say . . . twenty-eight, anyway. Today these are only semblances, let's not start allowing ourselves to be deceived. Do you follow, my good sir? Their existence is, at the very least, doubtful. Even a clock with no gears tells the correct time twice a day. Does that mean that it keeps track of the time, and that we ought to trust it?"

I don't know why, but the clock example convinced me. I understood why they don't ring at the Bernardines'. Down below, the stones were silent, because they had no one to speak to. They sank in the ever-deepening water, whose surface was getting closer to where we stood with every passing moment, pock-marked from the rain, in the image of the face of my priest. I couldn't figure out if the water was collecting, climbing towards us, or if we were falling to the depths, too heavy to soar. I wanted to thank the priest for saving me. But he and some others were already cutting the bells from their ropes and rolling them with a booming crash. One by one they thunderously splashed into the water. We had cut the excess ballast that was slowly pulling us down. The vast shoreless water grew calm a safe distance below us; we had surfaced correctly. The rain ceased.

'Cause He's Stupid, and 'Cause He's Abram

He had a molting beard the color of hempen harl, his frayed canvas clothes were made up of holes and cracks painstakingly sewn together. Niemira from Leśne claimed that Abram had stolen those rags from his field scarecrow and was now parading about in them. Possible, but if so, Stupid Abram hadn't taken them to make himself frightening, only so that he would have something to wear: without them he was already fairly frightening, though more naked.

He was most often silent, and prone to staring so far-sightedly he perhaps saw only those things that lie beyond the limits of the visible world. He would sit without moving, and on his half-open lips was a glassy spit-bubble, peering outwards like the sole watchful eye over his idiocy. Only the sight of blooming sunflowers could tear him from his stupor. Stupid Abram would stand behind the fence and ask with a stammering groan: "Mr. Famrer, would you give me a sunflowwwer . . ." He called everyone a "famrer," which no doubt meant "farmer." If his request was granted, Abram would grab the head of the sunflower with both hands and stare at it, holding it up to his eyes, as though counting the seeds or trailing some elusive bumblebee. After this inspection, smiling and mumbling to himself, he would sit behind the wall of the smithery and eat.

Rabbi Zawłodawer himself would say that Abram wasn't a man, he was a loss, that not even half a word of Gomorrah had entered his ears. The synagogue shammes was of a different opinion, he claimed that more than one of God's words got through to Abram's miserable mind, though he might not have entirely understood them. But who could say that he agreed with God in everything he was meant to? At harvest time, on all the days of the week except for market day, in deserted Zaręby, amidst the garbage stench rising in the heat, in the golden dust from the disintegrating horse manure, Stupid Abram became the sole attraction for the children blocking his way from all sides, throwing worm-eaten apples, shouting: "Abram, I'll play for you! Abram, I'll play for you! Abram, I'll play for you!"

And then Abram stopped, seeing that there was no way

out, and started dancing that hideous dance born of his fear, and it was all the more comical the more frightened he became. The children wrapped their fists into trumpets and they played. Abram's steps only seemed to be random and haphazard; his clumsy pirouettes served to guard him from clouts on the back, in his constant spinning he sought to have the entire surrounding danger in front of him; the flapping of his hands at eye level was no mere flourish, it was also a shield against the sudden impact of an apple or wild pear. Oh, the children knew that no one was as funny as Stupid Abram when he got scared! But his dance never went on for long, the hand trumpets fell silent one after another, choked with laughter. Abram grew still, and became frightening, much more frightening than before.

He stood still, and in this standing there was more haste than in the most feverish escape. The fear which had thus far grown out of Abram in whole swarms of flutters and a thicket of gesticulations now spread on all sides in short waves of breathlessness, a quivering of the air, an infection of panic. The ring of gawkers widened, the boys retreated one step at a time, and then Abram would slowly walk out of the circle, with no one trying to stop him, and each plodding step was an utterly concealed hop, a potential sprint, fettered by a clever imitation of calm. Only a few good moments later did Abram permit himself to escape, at the point where he could be reached only by the blow of a particularly well-aimed apple.

And then he could run and lament. Kicking up clouds of dust and wailing, Abram was soon behind the tombstones, running with a complaint that would receive no response, to the first houses he came across: to Gitla, to Małka, to Ester. They didn't care to listen to him, and anyway, what was there to hear? The women slammed their doors in his face; only Gitla: "Why did you dance? Were you that happy? Well, they hit you because they can tell you're stupid." So Abram has no one to moan to; he can't go to the parish, to the priest's housekeeper. He'll go home.

In the place where Zaręby gave onto the quaggy road to Uścianek, there stood a pair of synagogues: one was operating, the other had been burned to the ground sometime in the past and was left in ruins, to the bunches of grass and weeds growing even onto the tops of the red walls. The burned-out interior wasn't even fit for rebuilding and prayer. That was where Stupid Abram had his nest and overnight shelter. He reclined there, at home, among hundreds of deseeded sunflower heads lying on the ground and stuffed into the gaps between bricks, like great votive offerings to the Sun God. In the evening, the sun shone through the windows into this temple of Abram, and in the empty interior it swiftly built an illusionary bimah and gold-red Aron HaKodesh on the foundation of the shadows. It was at that hour precisely, when, passing by that spot, I heard Abram's monotonous muttering, but only God knows if it was a prayer.

Later on, I didn't see Stupid Abram for a few years, but that doesn't mean I knew any less about his life. For all those years that same past just repeated itself for him, multiplied intact in yearly installments, from spring to winter; those same worm-eaten apples fell from the trees, the seeds reposed in their sunflowers, and the foolish leaps were always the sure path to escape and salvation from the fear. I saw him only just before his first journey.

It was when the sunflowers were ripening. The whole square was full of carts at that early hour, as if it was market day, but the carts were empty, they were still empty. They had arrived here in the morning on a German order to collect all the Zaręby Jews and to transport them to Szulbor. Budziniak had come from there at dawn, whispering that the pits had all been made ready.

They left their cottages and one-story log cabins with their bundles, with their children, they clambered onto the carts, sometimes small fights erupted over who went where, they still didn't know the worst of it. The Germans were busy with their breakfasts, they didn't get involved. From afar I saw Stupid Abram, and for a moment I thought that maybe I would be able to warn him before they noticed him in the square, to turn him back to the old synagogue. As he walked he was giggling and arguing with himself. It was hard to understand Abram's words, but his gestures were clear. They showed joy above all, a joy which made Abram manifold, which multiplied him somehow into so many Abrams that they could barely find space inside of him. He wasn't speaking to himself, he was talking to all of them, to each Abram individually, quickly giving them some good bit of news. I figured that he was enjoying that crowd of Abrams who kept him from feeling lonely, sharing the joy that he wouldn't have been able to support on his own. What could I give him apart from some good advice and a sunflower?

"Don't go there, Abram, they'll catch you and you'll land . . ."

Abram stuffed the sunflower head under his shirt and stammered, more clearly than usual:

"In the Promised Land!"

He smiled triumphantly, nodding his head to show he was pleased, and maybe out of gratitude for the sunflower, nodding on and on, perhaps in the name of all the Abrams he had inside him. I saw that I would neither stop him nor convince him. That the old shammes was right when he said some of God's words were rattling about in Abram's barren memory, some words which went not entirely understood. Abram walked on, occupied with his secret discussions divided into a thousand gestures, he walked straight towards the approaching Germans, passing the first carts already on their way out, and in them: eyes, many black eyes, wide open to all the horror in the world.

The German's first blow landed Abram right in the center of a puddle, then a kick rolled him onto the pavement; Abram scrambled away on all fours and was about to stand up, when he saw Simche the Wise, lying on the ground and utterly lifeless. Abram studied him up close like he did sunflower seeds, clapped his hands, tore himself away, and was soon running with hobbling jumps toward the last cart, blood flowing from his wide grin. He jumped in and sat next to Gitla, who was beside the shammes himself.

"Oy! You stupid! You always dance till you get a beating," said Gitla, pressing her bundle tightly to her breast, no doubt intending to use it to set up a new household wherever they were going. "It's all because you're stupid."

"Oy!" cried Abram, wiping the blood from his face. "Oy! Maybe Simche is stupid too? Who says that Simche is stupid? Oh, there he lies!"

The cart passed by an outstretched and motionless body, to which Abram bid farewell with his index finger. When the caravan of carts left along the road to Uścianek, Abram pulled his sunflower out from his bosom and started rapidly pecking out seed after seed, almost birdlike, spitting out the shells, as if he didn't want to leave any for later on, for the journey's end: a land full of sunflower groves.

Waiting for the Dog to Sleep

I'm in an old doghouse, cramped up, my knees touching my chin. Through the gaps in the planks I see an expansive square, empty as far as the saplings bordering it. This used to be my village. Yesterday was the end of the demolition, the last shack was torn down, the villagers left in dozens of wagons for their new homes in the city. The area is supposed to be forested. I've hidden myself, I'm in the doghouse, I didn't want to leave.

The sun is still shining low in front of me, but I'm in the shadow of the watchdog, which is sitting stiffly balanced on his front legs, he hasn't slept for many hours, he's been trying not to sleep with all his might. I have faith in the dog's vigilance: it's the reason why I can sometimes doze off. I see the gamekeepers and the ranger still standing there: they are staring at the doghouse, the last one in this wasteland, they are waiting for the dog to sleep. Behind them tower heaps of forest saplings.

Sometimes the dog's head falls in mortal exhaustion. Then the gamekeepers come a few steps closer. The dog snaps back to alertness in the blink of an eye and bares his fangs, the gamekeepers back up beyond the chain's radius, and the dog bites into his own flank with a mouth gaping wide, warding off sleep with pain. And again he sits as straight as an effigy, eye to eye with the people. Once he kept watch over the property next door; since it's no longer there, he's only got himself to protect.

I don't know when I dozed off; again I was woken up. I see the dog baring his fangs and digging his teeth into his own body, I see the gamekeepers backing off to a safe distance. I hear: "Forest Ranger, sir, requesting permission please." "No," says the ranger, "For the time being you're not allowed. According to the statutes, stray dogs are shot in the woods. Let's wait: he'll fall asleep, we'll plant trees around him, and then."

The dog bites away the sleep, much as he once dove into the fleas tangled up in his curls. I'm grateful to him, though he doesn't even know that I'm here, in his house. It's broad daylight, but his eyelids are closing to the darkness of sleep.

I'm awoken by a brief whimper. It's the dog calling out

for the first and last time. The jaws sunk deeply into his body will never again part. The dog lies still: he has bitten away sleep to the death. From under his torn skin protrude stumps of broken ribs. Nothing is protecting me anymore, but it doesn't matter — to tell the truth, that hopeless dogged fight for survival was starting to irritate me, and my position in the doghouse has gotten tiresome as well; my whole neck and spine have stiffened and grown painfully numb. What's the point in staying, there's no village here anymore, better to move to the city, the gamekeepers are already tossing the dead dog to one side with the butts of their rifles; I'm going, I'll help them forest the place . . . Stretching my cramped legs, I demolish the doghouse from within. I leave, saying: "How about that, eh? I got lucky: that sure was a mad dog."

Post-Patrimony

When the house was left completely alone after their deaths, I shouldn't have gone by there, yet I couldn't resist the opportunity. The corners are deceptively similar, an effect that erodes with time. Even the recollections which bred here for years have fled the cold rooms like lice from a corpse. Since no one has been to visit, I have become a frequent guest there, I have come to observe the decaying process. Not long ago everything was holding together fine, propped up by the daily comings and goings. Even Grandfather's nocturnal snoring was a warning signal of his presence, a sign to make the objects understand that they were still obliged to serve.

Now there are no obligations. I don't count, I'm a stranger, I would be greeted by a chained barking, if there were a dog. Luckily my grandparents didn't know, or they couldn't have known the suspense with which everything around them had eagerly awaited their departure. With what relief their absence was received. The decay, stalled for years, could finally set in like a season, red like the autumn. It's not true that man causes destruction; abandoned places deteriorate more effectively on their own. Only Grandma's watch, a memento kept in a drawer, was never wound so as to be better preserved, and was thus rendered useless: the gears that were accustomed to the flow of time have silted up.

I came again. I took a short cut: the fence has been pilfered, winding paths lead through the trampled flowerbeds. Burdocks tangle themselves under the window: there are whole mobs of them, listening for the right moment to march in. I'm in the living room with the remains of a plush tablecloth, an iron pounding overhead. The neighbors' children are throwing green apples at the roof, which is covered in rusted sheet metal. For these things left to their own devices, the clanging completes the rite of self-annihilation.

Nobody stops by here, only blind Dobek. There he is standing behind the remains of the fence, waiting like he used to when he brought the milk.

"I see that you're here," says blind Dobek. "I bring two

liters to the Pacul family. The old couple used to take three. Do I see that you're renovating?"

"No."

"But will you?"

"I don't know, it's possible," I lie. "Mr. Dobek, please bring me four liters for the evening."

"A fine house is a fine house!" says Dobek, and as he walks away, he throws in, "I swear on Grandma's red britches."

I assumed he had got this from Grandpa and then adopted his eternal stock phrase, which, unbearable though it may have been for Grandma, had more and more often escaped her attention as the years made her deaf. Dobek would often say with admiration that my grandfather had principles which had somehow held everything in the house together. It had held together all right, but Grandpa had no secrets apart from living his life, a life of his own. And after all, he did hold himself together for a long time and fairly well; he was a pragmatist with no routines, unless Dobek counted that daily oath involving Grandma and her red britches. I myself don't know if it was sincere, but I am sure that it didn't mean much. Repeated day after day, it grew threadbare and faded, as senseless as any common claptrap. Grandfather believed in the permanence of the table, the plush amaranth tablecloth, the windows that were sealed for winter; this was well worth the trouble, and worth some carefully weighed and sober words. Yet sometimes, after his rounds of the house and garden to make certain that everything was holding together, he would take a fishing rod, go for a few hours to a nearby river in which swam no fish, and return home with his hook torn off.

All that was long ago, and it's hard to believe from where I stand today. I'm not sure if my aunts made any efforts on behalf of the further fate of the house. They live in a far-off city, they have their own apartments, which they are diligently domesticating, day by day, they held their homes in piety with needlepoint votives. And anyway, even if they gave some thought to their patrimony . . . What of it? The house is already annexed: when the rumbling of the sheet metal fades, you can hear the loose pulsations of the rotting wood, the sign of a new order. Oblivion, too, must settle itself in, with haste, with one eye on the present. It, too, is mortal, after all. I hear the patient burdocks nuzzling against the wall with every gust of wind. No longer overseen by Grandfather's steady watch, time is catching up in a hurry. Outside, the chirping of the grasshoppers is marking out time for the burdocks and weeds, a time that for now has no access to this house. In the living room, where I have been sitting for some hours, there is still a microclimate common to deserted places, in which the minutes and hours drop as imperceptibly as weightless husks.

For ages the walls have been holding themselves up on

their last legs, terrorized by the grandfatherly life, hammered to the spot by Grandmother's tread. Now the beams are silently splitting open, their very cores are being revealed, showing the overhanging wood's flabby sinews, exhaling its final breath in clouds of red dust. From one of those yawning cracks right by the door, three spoons made of tsarist silver fall at my feet with a clatter, spoons that Grandmother had written off after a fruitless search one evening dozens of years ago. Teaspoons! Now! I quickly store them in my pocket.

Incidentally, there is something shameless in this last gesture of the homestead's demise; there is a complete forfeiture of dignity, and an utter debauchery in the way it puffs out and spreads itself open wide, in the creaking yelps of the floorboards. And here of all places, where no mirror has ever reflected anything indecent!

My eyes were playing tricks. I had never before seen such scandalous, vaudevillian agony. Such leering of blind knotholes, such huffing and puffing of rotten wood, such sauntering annihilation! Maybe the house had good intentions. I wouldn't want to condemn the home of my ancestors once and for all. Maybe it had just been a question of tasteless appearances, a result of time feverishly rushing and tumbling down a steep slope. Maybe if time was running at normal speed, everything that was now unfolding in ticklish spasms would be happening in solemnity, in all the stateliness of its old age? Like the way old silent films, despite all their finest intentions, fall helplessly into unintended self-parody when sped up by modern projectors. Whatever the case, I couldn't merely sit back and watch.

My eyes were playing tricks. Even those post-Grandfather remains, those godforsaken fixtures sank into the dusk. Into the green dusk. I looked towards the window: it was the burdocks! The burdocks were overgrowing the house, reaching higher and higher, changing the windows into dark green stained glass.

I run outside. A black clamorous smoke is rising from the dead chimney: it is several generations of terrified jack-daws. Yes, the final moment has come, the house is getting swallowed up by the earth, or in fact it is sinking, gradually losing its contours, until it vanishes. The linden tree, the house's neighbor of eighty years, seems much taller than it did before, it's rustling normally, just like it always used to when it took the wind into its branches, as if nothing has happened. It is irreversible, and to think I wanted to avert it all with those four stupid liters of milk from blind Dobek! To make all the things believe I had Grandfather's foresight, that I was continuing someone else's life!

Now I know everything: for now the burdocks reign beneath the linden, as sure of their place as my grandparents were. But everything will start anew, because there are always roots left behind. Why did I take those spoons? They might clink once more in glasses of tea that

Grandma will set on the table. I sat on the chimney stack, jutting out from the earth like a giant molehill, and recalling all things bygone that await us, I threw the three silver spoons into it, one by one.

They didn't even ring out in the depths, everything was still, stripped of sound like in an old film. And then that murmur and patter! I took a look: the one tiny thing spared from the house was running through the thicket of burdocks, in scanty raspberry colored clothing, nodding her head with her bun untied. She had somehow ducked out, she alone. The burdocks tickle her with their hairy leaves. She leaps through and over them like an acrobat, the eternally young grandmother in the red britches I had heard so much about.

Stumps

By the wall and on the sidewalk, right next to the fruit-seller's display, sat a beggar, his two stumps stitched up in their pants legs and stretched out in front of him. I could have passed him, actually, by going straight ahead. But I had to make a detour: I avoided his ex-legs, I walked a wide arc around where his heels would have been. I didn't want to take advantage of a catastrophe, I could not sanction that well-aimed grenade by stepping straight on ahead.

And then the beggar suddenly hurled a curse at me, along with his cap filled with the coins he had gathered, which jingled as they hit the sidewalk. Could I have guessed that with my silent protest to his handicap I would be recreating his useless legs in imaginary boots, legs which ridiculed his powerlessness?

I hurried on without looking back. I was certain he would somehow pick up his daily earnings; sympathetic passersby would help him as they walked across the flagstones where his legs ought to have been. It was a sunny day, the spring smelled of car exhaust and lily of the valley. Girls in flowery skirts were strolling through the park, not even motherhood weighing them down. I was by myself, having just returned to the country, and in my stroll about town a single goal shone in my mind: to find at least one familiar face to prove that this was in fact a return. For the time being my only consolation was a peacock's-tail oil stain on the wet asphalt, an urban flight-less rainbow curled up in a ball beside the gutter. Rainbows have always lifted my spirits: my superstitions always came in colors.

I was putting off visiting Roman's family, or rather their home, their onetime apartment; I heard it had been spared. Finally, after an uneventful walk, I went to Wielka Street. The building was standing, half preserved, one of few left on the even-numbered side. A bomb had sliced it right down the middle, opening up the colorful interiors of apartments on all the floors. Dangling over the precipice, tiled stoves clung harrowingly to pink, green, and multi-colored walls. This public display of colorful intimacy wouldn't have spun my head had it not been for the green wall on the second floor, a wall with a narrow door but no stove. I had been there before, in that green, on those heights. Roman's grandmother got sick and it was said that the green room was getting at her, that the paint contained some kind of toxic substances. Grandmother was firmly convinced that the color itself would drag her to her grave, that it was a German color. Apparently she survived her whole family and died in Radom, after it was all over.

Now the stairs (I remember: on the left as you went in) were gone, so I got in by the kitchen ones, which weren't the slightest bit damaged even though they were made of wood. Even the reddish oil paint on the handrails had held up fairly well. I stood in front of a door on which the initials of the Three Kings were written in chalk. There was no point in going further. The chalk hadn't been touched, the lock was new. In the remainder of the apartment, minus its green room, someone had set up house, someone was filling up the abandoned space, which for them had been merely empty. The smell of potato pancakes frying in oil happily neighbored the abyss.

I ran down the stairs. The streets were covered in piles of rubble. You almost needed mountaineering skills to cross their sheer passes. And again homes, homes with partly-glazed windows. In one of them a woman was washing the glass. From under her upturned skirt peeked muscular, frost-bitten legs, visible to the base of her thighs. I paused: this was finally something. An everlasting ritual and a familiar species of a woman for all seasons, as appetizing as bread rations in days of hunger. She played out her mime show for me, the sole passerby, her hand gripping a rag as though it were a bouquet. When she stopped washing for a moment and returned my stare, I went away. After the morning rain the heat was unearthing the old smell of burning and decay from under the rubble. On a wall nearby, someone had written: "I'm on Karolkowa Street, Staszek + family in Grodzisko — Mietek."

Behind me there was a rumbling, quick and clamorous. It was my legless beggar riding on top of a board attached to iron wheels. With one hand he paddled and pushed himself clear of the sidewalk, and with the other he shook his fist. I began to escape along the street, leaping over the bricks tumbling off the heaps onto the cleared road. He must have been lurking in wait for me as I was occupied with the woman in the window. He was flinging pieces of bricks at me, no doubt for my four legs this time, for my over-abundance: two of my own and the woman's pair, the sight of which I had feasted on. What could I do? Everything, like it or not, pointed to his handicap, to such a degree that it was surprising he still hadn't grown used to it. I ran quickly through a pile of rubble that he wouldn't be able to cross. I had escaped on my stolen legs, but not from the chase: from the stumps.

And once again, out of breath, I found myself in front of Roman's building. I sat down on the bricks and lit a

Triumph cigarette. At a certain moment a terrifying creak reverberated from high above. The door in the green wall on the second floor slowly opened. On the threshold dividing the apartment from the precipice sat a boy, who started blowing soap bubbles from a straw. They bulged out and flew away, going rainbow-colored in the sun, in greens and violets, before disappearing into the unknown expanse of air.

Signs of the Times, or Diction

There came a time when I went away, I had lots of things to take care of, I remember saying *Wait till I return* or something like that. Then I had some ups and downs, everything except myself came and went, even my memories of it all. I recall only the moment of my departure, their nodding heads, that they would wait, for certain they would.

I remember the doorknob best, cool and brass, I held it for a long time in my hand before I left. Doorknobs are easy to remember. And now that I'm back at last, I am grateful to the doorknob for its immutability, for its patient loyalty to its form, to which my memory has also proven to be loyal. I ring the bell, I knock — no one opens the door.

Then I remember: I have the key, or I ought to, yes, it rattles in my pocket. The lock, by now unused to my key, opens with a weary groan.

No one's home. The room is full of their absence, it has settled in well, faded and fragrant with mustiness. In the fraying air the objects are all clothed in gray. Eleonora's slipper sits on the windowsill, misshapen from the constant disuse, a little hunchback burdened with the comical proportions of its own misfortune. It lingers in its archaic elegance, ridiculed by time. The lengthwise cobwebs glimmer with thousands of moth wings.

I am vainly searching for a trace, a message, a note, a couple of words from which I could gather that they had had to leave and give up waiting. The sadness of such a confirmation would soothe the anxiety that they had waited to the bitter end. There is nothing, not a single word for me among the immemorial scraps, which I pull out from under the loose and gray plush covering everything around me.

So what if I once asked for patience? Was my request so binding? You can wait with a faraway presence at your side. But what if, bound to the moment of my departure, they have remained in that time past, antiquated and inaccessible? And I kept telling them: you have to move, for Christ's sake, movement is essential, a bit of fresh air, a bit of anything, not like that, not like that! I don't want to believe my eyes: almost nothing remains of the old furniture, of either the cupboard, or the trunks, or the demijohn with the cherry liqueur. They have moved, clearly they have moved.

Only the doorknob corresponds to my flashbacks, but I can't stay for its sake alone. I open the door. This raises a cloud of dust. Awoken by the stir of air, a scrap of paper rustles in the corner. I recognize my own handwriting, it's my letter to Eleonora. She didn't even bother to take it with her. I brush the dust from the letter and read: "My Beloved Eleonora! I recall thee to my mind, whenever I behold thy flower . . ."

Thus I have returned to the past, but I have gone too far, way too far. No wonder: it's easy to lose one's way in the past, in exhausted time, cut adrift from any chronology, where the further you get the more blurred everything becomes.

Good God! Where did he get this diction? What flower was he talking about? Who was this Eleonora of his, apart from her outdated name? What did she look like? Had I seen even a daguerreotype of her, I would surely have remembered her, as I have the doorknob. I stop reading, who needs other people's secrets. There's no doubt: something has passed someone by. And I no longer ask myself where to, to what times, in which direction and for whom the past is lost.

Spinning Circles

A hoop is an ordinary thing, a child's toy, a slender band made to turn with a stick, steadily rotating ahead, straight ahead. If I run after it, if I press it onwards and guard it from mishap, I do this not for fun — I've long since left childhood — but from a compulsion, born from what was once free-willed recklessness. I wanted to get to the City, to my father's home. I could not permit myself, however, a mere peregrination, a flagrant pursuit, consumed only by the desire to reach my goal. They would have stopped me before I reached the tollgate, recognizing me as an outlaw, cast out long ago by the City authorities.

Yet I had to return. Each year supplied me with

alarming evidence that the climate of the rural plains did not agree with me. I observed the following symptoms: graying around the temples, protruding knots of veins, and a proneness to asthma that only grew with the passing of time, with the onrush of time. I took my wooden hoop with its old inscription, "Franio," a hoop that had once been my toy, and I set out along the road of my childhood, in this way somehow merging with the traffic, all in the hope that I would be overlooked by the City sentries.

It's already dusk. The road whitens before my eyes, it runs as straight as an arrow. I am running, lightly tapping along the hoop so that the rotations don't slow down, not out of hurry, but concern that if it were to lose momentum it would spin sluggishly to quiescence. The forest on both sides of the road appears to secure the proper direction, not permitting the slightest deviation from the straight course. Behind the roadside junipers dazzling scraps of sunlight lie scattered here and there in the darkness, not having managed to escape the brushwood with the oncoming twilight. A whole flock of puffed up and twittering birds are warming themselves in the archipelago of light. As I pass by, my hoop's shadow stretches itself out on the road, ellipsoidal and elastic, the hoop's inscription falls under my eyes time and again, rhythmically, only visible for a few moments: "Franio" — "Franio" — "Franio" — till I am immersed once more in the darkness. I took heart: I am a man from the plains, unaccustomed to landscapes rolling with hills and valleys, a horizon that does not know the perfection of a circle. I must remain true to my course.

The forests ended, the moon began, and everything turned smooth and white like my road. I feel no fatigue. I don't know if this is because I'm approaching my father's house, or because all of my attention is concentrated on guiding the hoop and maintaining its balance, leaving me free to take deep invigorating breaths. The lights of the City, still somewhere beyond the horizon, paint the patch of skyline before me in the redness of a counterfeit sunrise. This is my point of orientation, my hope. In this radiance, there must be the light shining from my father's window: He is waiting up for me, I'm sure of it. So I am spinning the hoop through the illuminated night, my trusty hoop. It hasn't let me down, in our shared pursuit it has merited the faith held in the rotation of the earth; it is infallible.

The highest lights are already peeking out from behind the earth, quivering and pointed, but somehow too far to the left, decidedly too far. As if a sparkling and illuminated battleship has unmoored itself from the horizon and started slowly to drift away. I must have made an error: My hoop is deviating slightly to the right! I try to correct its path; I tap it on the right, but it stubbornly spins along some wrong track, and my intervention only risks a loss of balance. I know I would have no right to lift it off the ground, that the journey would end once and for all, that I must — we must — run without cease. Those few dozen centimeters are hardly a catastrophe, after all! Let's not get carried away, we're not traveling exactly the way we ought to, but we are nonetheless getting nearer to the City. Are we really getting closer? Is the hoop now irretrievably drifting off course? But even if so, what could be more unswerving than the law of geometry, than the inevitable separation of the two arms of a razor-sharp angle? A scarcely perceptible imperfection, the error of a mere centimeter in measurement and the separation grows like a landslide, multiplies into miles, and then hundreds of miles. Now, by this point already, in order to see the lights of the City I have to steal glances over my left shoulder. It's as though at my journey's end an irresistible current were carrying me further and further from the already visible shoreline, into the darkness.

A low quivering light appears in the dusk: I'm not alone, it's coming closer and closer. It's a kerosene lamp hanging from the side of a wagon. It isn't heading straight towards the City either, or so it seems. The coachman is nodding off on his platform, his shiny-brimmed hat pressed down low onto his forehead. Suddenly he is awoken by my mother screaming from behind him: "Mr. Sokołowski! For the love of God, let's not go tipping into a ditch!" "Giddyup!" cries Sokołowski, and the horses turn towards the City. "Mama," I cry, "Tell Father that I'm trying my hardest . . ." I stop short, for the wagon was no longer there. I must have been running perpendicular to my original road, the acute angle has at least straightened out, if it wasn't obtuse. And again I hear the voice from out of the darkness: "I will wear holes in these shoes before I get there, they will be completely useless." And the response: "Are you suggesting again, Uncle, that I should buy you another pair? If you didn't drink so much you'd have something to buy them with." This was the voice of Uncle Olek, Oleander, and his niece replying. Oleander, drunk as usual, was reeling about but somehow blundering his way to the City. No doubt he would get there, he didn't follow straight lines.

I know I will never make it. I know with all my heart, like my lungs know the air they breathe, that my lot is no more than an inevitable service to the circle, though I wretchedly pretend to guide it. I have not once turned to the rear or even to the side; my retreat — for I am now running in precisely the opposite direction, the City steadily diminishing behind my back — happened unawares as I kept moving forwards. Father, if you were waiting up, don't take it the wrong way. Believe me, it's not my fault that as I was running to you I fell into this remoteness unawares, whereupon you and your house and the City, which has now completely vanished from sight, would become unimaginable. After all, you know that your son is a Circle Spinner.

What have I got left apart from despair? One thing: the search for meaning, which rests on the hope that someday the hoop, in its complex meanderings, will perhaps stumble its way to where it doesn't want to arrive: the City. To help it out, my misguided chase grew wings of new significance; my ring will keep its circular shape only provided that it spins, that it never ceases its rotations. Its natural movement is like a lathe in constant movement, a confirmation of form. For the shape of the circle and the notion of circling are, essentially, one and the same. Yes, unable to become the captain and dictator of the circle, I somehow became its caretaker. I would not have confessed this new faith or my new role to anyone. I would have feared that, had I entrusted them to anyone, they would have lost their credibility. Let this truth remain exclusively mine. I'll lie to other people if I have to.

Day is already breaking. The world is not yet deserving of colors, though it has separated itself into light and shade. I don't care about the landscape I'm passing: It's whatever it is, which is how things should be, it serves only for traveling through, I expect nothing from it. Thus the procession heading in the opposite direction, though it is still far off, is as unexpected as it is indifferent. The faces, recognized only at close proximity, fill me with anxiety. What could I tell them? . . . My hoop has been spinning perfectly since I stopped tending to its balance and direction, turning faultlessly on its axel of air. What could I tell them?

I see our old maid Lodka, Krystosiak, Uncle Romek, and leading the pack is Doctor Trenkner, whom I was never afraid of because he sweetened his pediatric checkups with multicolored candies. He recognized me and called out: "Hey Franio! Out playing so early?" "Yes, Doctor. For my health, Doctor." I had already passed him, but he still threw in: "Come with us to the City for a little breakfast." "Later. I'm going to play a bit more."

Now, when every step is carrying me a step further from the City, and there have perhaps already been one thousand thousand of these steps, it is pointless to keep spinning the hoop, I realize this. Running is none too easy when you're trampling your own hopes as you go. But it's not just that the hoop needs me, I need it too. It's the last keepsake of my childhood, and it, too, is a stray exile from the City. I've had to renounce everything, and now am I expected to give up the one thing I've got left? I am a Circle Spinner. You can keep on spinning, after all, even when all hope is lost, even when the horizon has come to nothing, at least you can believe in a hoop, an old wooden hoop with an inscription that reads "Franio," believe in it and show it kindness, especially on this road full of potholes and stones.

Now we are traveling, my hoop and I, through a forest. It's hard to weave through the trunks, and worst of all are the pine roots jutting up from the earth. My strength has abandoned me, I seem to be growing weaker with each passing second: the piercing scoff of a woodpecker sends the stick flying from my hand. The hoop falls first, overcome by my swoon. Then it's my turn, curled up, shrunken almost to the size of an embryo, I lie in the very center of the hoop, at the foot of some yellow helichrysums, in the shadow of a scabiosa swaying under the weight of a burnet moth. Wherever I turn my gaze my landscape ends at the horizon of the hoop, a wooden horizon. Nearby, old Lodka is spinning a long thread from a spider with the quick one-two jerks of a milkmaid. Uncle Oleander, drunk as a skunk, is doing log rolls in the thyme, spooking the bumblebees. And then Mother: "Well finally! Father has been waiting for ages! . . ." "I'm coming, Mama!" I feel good, I'm smiling at everything above me. In the sky the sun's disk painstakingly and faultlessly spins towards its zenith.

Translator, poet, ethnologist, philosophy graduate, impromptu soldier, entomologist, collector of oddities, lyricist, and devotee as well as biographer of Bruno Schulz, Jerzy Ficowski also wrote short stories for a brief period, a genre he has never returned to and — by his own reckoning — never will. This burst of narrative creativity was collected under the title *Waiting for the Dog to Sleep*, which was very well-received, went through a few editions, and then disappeared from bookstores. It is still out of print today, despite assurances from the Polish publishing house Pogranicze that they will release Ficowski's entire output to date in new editions (Ficowski was named "Pogranicze Person of the Year" some time ago, and now the publishing house is "taking care of him.") Thus, the only way to get one's hands on the Polish edition of *Waiting* is by digging through plenty of used-book stores, and being very patient.

English-language readers may be familiar with Ficowski through his volume of poetry *A Reading of Ashes*, but more likely via *Regions of the Great Heresy* (his "biographical portrait" of Bruno Schulz) or his various forewords to editions of Schulz in English, and if so they will be expecting *Waiting* to be brimming with Schulziana of all sorts — and may be surprised at how little is to be found. Doubtless there are traces: the descriptions of chestnuts in "Recreation with the Paralytics," the odd relationship between the narrator and Miss Firanelli in "An Attempt at a Dialogue" (more reminiscent of Schulz's drawings than his stories) or the way childhood memories translate into a sinister magic in "The Sweet Smell of Wild Animals." But the overwhelming impression is that every one of Ficowski's attempts to lift into ecstatic Schulzian heights ends in inertia and silence, every attempt to reach back into the past proves futile, and mythology, the stuff of Schulz's narratives, is barren or impossible.

This transition strikes me not so much as a literary tactic, but as an honest attempt to reconcile literature with a reality that had changed beyond recognition. Ficowski participated in the Warsaw Uprising, and witnessed the annihilation of Warsaw, the city where he grew up. His narrators are constantly, obsessively in search of something to link the past to the present ("The Pink House," "Outskirts on the Sands," "Gorissia," "Stumps"), struggling to establish some sort of continuum to reality. This "reality," I believe, should be understood as physical (i.e. the landscape), emotional (memories and personal history), and literary (tradition). *Waiting*'s interwoven metaphors, then, are extremely slippery, and Ficowski is at pains to keep historical contexts as murky and indistinct as possible, with a few exceptions ("'Cause He's Stupid, and 'Cause He's Abram" clearly addresses the Holocaust, while "Intermission" is obviously about the Warsaw Uprising).

Ficowski brings his various expertises to bear in *Waiting*, and obviously all the specialist insect and plant names (some of which turn out to be invented), words associated with Judaic and Polish Catholic ritual and concentration-camp slang caused translation problems. And then, of course, there is the simple fact of the enormity of Ficowski's vocabulary, and his penchant for archaic or seldom-encountered words, or words more properly belonging to the Russian language (from which he has translated Leśmian into Polish). Finally, Ficowski is first and foremost a poet, and in the shortest stories ("Old-World Entomology," "Mimesis," "The Joy of Dead Things") this is well in evidence. These stories tend to abandon beginning-middle-end narrative strategy and have more to do with atmosphere, rendered above all by stretching language, working the language's paradoxes against itself. Finding equivalents for some of these passages, somehow doing justice to the writing's atmosphere, has been one of the great trials (and joys) of translating this book.

To conclude, a brief anecdote. After getting in contact with Ficowski, now eighty years old, Marcin and I drove from Cracow to Warsaw to visit him, at his invitation. In a room covered in Schulz's drawings, Roma dolls, insects and other objects that would make the Quay brothers green with envy (an exhibit was arranged in 1999 in Sejny called "The Cabinet of Jerzy Ficowski," displaying some of the unusual things he keeps in his home), Ficowski explained to us the derivation of the stories in *Waiting*, one by one. After explaining "The Pink House," he mentioned that the house in question was destroyed during the war, but that another pink building was built in the same spot shortly thereafter. With more enthusiasm than common sense, we asked him for the address so that we could go visit the place. And despite his protests that there was nothing to see, he eventually shrugged his shoulders and told us the address.

When we left him we did go in search of the Pink House, and

though it took us half an hour we eventually got there. The Pink House we eventually saw was a shiny metal high-rise with a massive mobile phone advertisement stretched across the length of it, so that the pinkness was only just visible, peeking out from underneath. Moral: literature ought not to be taken too literally, and in the competition between literature and reality, reality will always come off the poorer.

Thanks are in order to, above all, my co-translator Marcin Piekoszewski, whose insight is peerless, as well as Howard Sidenberg, Scotia Gilroy and Caitlin Gilroy for their perceptive comments. Thanks are also due the editors of the *Chicago Review*, *Metamorphoses*, the *Prague Literary Review*, *Snow Monkey*, *Absinthe*, and *Transfusion* for publishing earlier versions of these stories in their pages.

Soren A. Gauger
Cracow, 2006

p. 18 *Cholera epidemics* . . . : In Polish the word "cholera" used colloquially is roughly the equivalent of "dammit."

p. 21 *Emil Wedel* (1841-1919): Famous chocolate and candy manufacturer. Products from his factory were sold all across Europe and are still being made in Poland today. Wedel's flamboyant signature appears large on all his products.

p. 23 *pampuszki*: Small buns that are a favorite of Ukrainian cuisine.

p. 24 *Champollion*: Jean Francois Champollion (1790-1832) was a French egyptologist, the first to decipher the Egyptian hieroglyphics.

p. 25 *January Uprising*: A national uprising (1863-64) against the Russians, one of the three partitioning forces to which Poland lost its independence in 1795 (the partition lasted over one hundred years).

p. 27 *rorarty service*: A Catholic mass in honor of the Holy Virgin Mary, held in the Advent season just before Christmas.

p. 36 *Ostrowia Mazowiecka*: A town in Eastern Poland. Presently Ostrów Mazowiecka.

p. 43 *Bieszczady Mountains*: A mountain range in South-Eastern Poland, bordering the Ukraine and Slovakia. The Użocka Pass divides the Bieszczady into its Western (Polish) and Eastern (Ukrainian) parts.

p. 49 *Tango Milonga*: One of Poland's biggest dance-hall hits of all time, the song was first performed in 1928 by Stanisława Nowicka. It was exported to Vienna the following year with its name changed to "Oh, Donna Clara?"

p. 54 *Pelcowizna*: Before the Second World War a poor blue-collar neighborhood in Warsaw.

p. 60 *kvas*: A sour drink made of salt water and yeast.

p. 109 *pierogi*: Small dough dumplings usually filled with meat, potato, or cabbage.

p. 126 *Brzesko-Kujawska Culture*: A culture that developed in the 4th and 3rd millennia BCE in the region of what is today central-northern Poland. The dead were buried in an unusual position, with their legs tucked under.

p. 128 *Sieradz*: A town in central Poland. Traces of the first settlements from the Sieradz region hail from the 6th-7th centuries CE.

Jerzy Ficowski was born in 1924 in Warsaw and is a distinguished poet, prose writer, scholar and translator (from Yiddish, Russian, and Roma). During the German occupation of Warsaw in World War II, he served in the Home Army (AK) and took part in the Warsaw Uprising of 1944. He has published about twenty volumes of poetry since his debut in 1948 and one book of short stories: *Waiting for the Dog to Sleep*. His poetry has been illustrated by Marc Chagall, and his 1979 collection of poems, *A Reading of Ashes*, has been called the most moving account of the Holocaust written by a non-Jew. A major scholar of Roma history and culture (his book *Gypsies in Poland: History and Customs* is seminal), he has translated Roma folk tales into Polish (*Sister of the Birds and Other Gypsy Tales*), and is one of the most active translators of Yiddish literature remaining in Poland.

Since 1946 Ficowski has dedicated a vast amount of time to reassembling the scattered fragments of the visual and literary legacy of Bruno Schulz, a writer of great importance whose work was under-appreciated following the Second World War. At the time of its publication in Polish, Ficowski's "biographical portrait," *Regions of the Great Heresy* (W. W. Norton, 2003), was groundbreaking, and it remains the definitive study of Schulz's life and artistic legacy. Instrumental in establishing the collection of Schulziana at the Adam Mickiewicz Museum of Literature in Warsaw and in planning the permanent Schulz Museum in Drohobycz, Ukraine, Ficowski has edited varoius compilations of Schulz's letters and drawings and wrote the introduction to *The Drawings of Bruno Schulz*. He lives in Warsaw.

ABOUT THE TRANSLATORS

Soren A. Gauger is from Vancouver, Canada and lives in Cracow, Poland. He writes a regular column for the city's cultural monthly *Miesiąc w Krakowie* and is the in-house translator for *2+3D*, Poland's only design quarterly. His own writing and translations of Polish fiction have appeared in a number of publications. He is the author of a collection of stories, *Hymns to Millionaires* (Twisted Spoon Press, 2004), and a chapbook, *Quatre Regards sur l'Enfant Jésus.*

Marcin Piekoszewski was born in 1973 in Kluczbork, Poland. He studied at the English Departments of Opole University and Cracow's Jagiellonian University, graduating from the latter with a degree in American Literature. He has worked as a teacher, translator, journalist, and bookseller. He currently resides in Berlin.

WAITING FOR THE DOG TO SLEEP

by Jerzy Ficowski

Translated by Soren A. Gauger & Marcin Piekoszewski
from the Polish original *Czekanie na sen psa*
(Kraków: Wydawnictwo Literackie, 1970)

Design by Jed Slast
Set in Janson
Cover image and frontispiece by Jan Raczkowski

This is a first edition published in 2006 by
TWISTED SPOON PRESS
P.O. Box 21—Preslova 12, 150 21 Prague 5, Czech Republic
info@twistedspoon.com / www.twistedspoon.com

We gratefully acknowledge the editors of the following
publications for printing earlier versions of the stories:
*Chicago Review, Metamorphoses, Prague Literary Review,
Snow Monkey, Absinthe, Transfusion*

Distributed in North America by
SCB DISTRIBUTORS
15608 South New Century Drive
Gardena CA, 90248
toll free: 1-800-729-6423
info@scbdistributors.com / www.scbdistributors.com

Printed and bound in the Czech Republic
by Tiskárny Havlíčkův Brod